For Jamie st
Family -
Thanks for being
Ewheesma people!

John H. Bidwell

FUSHEESWA

John H. Bidwell

BALBOA.
PRESS

A DIVISION OF HAY HOUSE

Author Photo by Vicki Haggerty.

Scripture quotations are from The Holy Bible, English Standard Version® (ESV®), copyright © 2001 by Crossway, a publishing ministry of Good News Publishers. Used by permission. All rights reserved.

This is a work of fiction. All of the characters, names, incidents, organizations, and dialogue in this novel are either the products of the author's imagination or are used fictitiously.

Balboa Press books may be ordered through booksellers or by contacting:

Balboa Press
A Division of Hay House
1663 Liberty Drive
Bloomington, IN 47403
www.balboapress.com
1 (877) 407-4847

Because of the dynamic nature of the Internet, any web addresses or links contained in this book may have changed since publication and may no longer be valid. The views expressed in this work are solely those of the author and do not necessarily reflect the views of the publisher, and the publisher hereby disclaims any responsibility for them.

The author of this book does not dispense medical advice or prescribe the use of any technique as a form of treatment for physical, emotional, or medical problems without the advice of a physician, either directly or indirectly. The intent of the author is only to offer information of a general nature to help you in your quest for emotional and spiritual well-being. In the event you use any of the information in this book for yourself, which is your constitutional right, the author and the publisher assume no responsibility for your actions.

Any people depicted in stock imagery provided by Thinkstock are models, and such images are being used for illustrative purposes only.
Certain stock imagery © Thinkstock.

Print information available on the last page.

ISBN: 978-1-5043-8152-9 (sc)
ISBN: 978-1-5043-8153-6 (hc)
ISBN: 978-1-5043-8154-3 (e)

Library of Congress Control Number: 2017908391

Balboa Press rev. date: 06/02/2017

Contents

1

The Dream

A green luminescent curtain of clouds rippled before him, glowing, and he felt himself pushed into it. It had to be the aurora borealis, but it is impossible to get this close to it. The ground beneath him felt more solid than rock, but what could that mean? He felt a strange absence of fear, and still felt pushed. He was moving through whatever this was until suddenly there was a sound which seemed to come from everywhere. It was a faint rushing sound, perhaps a waterfall, perhaps it was everything breathing. The colorful world around him seemed blurred at first, but slowly came in to focus as if he had been looking through a camera lens. He found himself in a place alive with colorful plants, insects, flowers, motion. There was a mist as far as the eye could see. John could not see the ground he was standing on, but now it felt soft. He could see a stream to his left, and both sides of a path before him were lined with ferns. The mist moved across from left to right at about his knee level, a gentle breeze waving it like a huge curtain. He was always mindful of his breathing, like he was receiving the gift of air, but he was surprised he could not sense the moisture or any coolness in his nostrils or lungs. For some reason he could not feel his breathing at all.

"Perhaps a clue," he spoke softly to himself. Whenever he faced some mystery he imagined that he filed it in his mind under the title "Clue." He let things mystify him with a rather firm suspicion the strangest of pieces may find a clear place in the puzzle eventually. Don't force them.

He lifted his right leg until he could see his shoe above the moist curtain and slowly rotated his leg counter clockwise in an attempt to stir the mist, but he seemed to have no effect on his surroundings. He stepped forward and walked along the path. The ferns seemed a lighter green than they should. One had the cutest tiny green frog on one of its leaves. He bent over to stare at it.

"Hi guy." It had bright red eyes. All the colors here seemed so sharp. A single water drop from somewhere above landed on the frog, a one drop shower was all that was needed. The frog used a big foot as a squeegee, sweeping the moisture away in an instant. This place was enchanting indeed.

The rushing sound did get louder as he progressed along the path, and the stream flowed more quickly. It must be a waterfall. The path gave way to a boardwalk. He slowly began to see his feet again as he walked along and the boardwalk rose above the mist. Now to either side there were rock formations, walls of slate outcrops lined with ferns and colorful mushrooms, orange, red, and leafy green plants with purple stripes. They seemed to almost glow. He could see the boardwalk led to a series of huge staircases going up the side of a mountain. After just the first set of stairs he stopped and looked down. It was an amazing view. He felt a real sense of accomplishment in the height he had attained, but there was so far to go. He counted the stairs as he climbed. He climbed twenty five stairs and then walked along a straight course over the boardwalk and then there was another twenty five stairs. He repeated the process over and over again. He wondered if he would complete a circle of this area in a day. He also noticed he was not getting tired. "Not bad for forty five years old," he thought. There was no heavy breathing, no rapid heartbeat, no leg pain or strain of any kind. How could this be? "Another clue," he whispered.

After perhaps an hour of meandering his way, checking out all manner of plants, and even a green lizard, he could see the waterfall. The water drops sparkled in the sunshine. Almost like shooting stars. Looking down at one angle he could see a rainbow. The colors, the ferns, the pines with their sacred fragrance, this was magical. He stood in awe. Finally it looked like there were only three sets of stairs and boardwalks to go. He could make out the top, and there appeared to be someone up there. He still did not feel strained in the least but he noticed he was walking more slowly. He hardly looked where he was going, but instead strained to see the figure at the end of this journey. The figure appeared feminine, and angelic, and the closer he approached the more she seemed of both. He could not feel his heart beating faster, but he somehow knew it was. How beautiful could she be? How beautiful can anybody be?

If his nurse could be believed John was quite a handsome catch. For the first time he could remember he found himself especially hoping his nurse was right about that. She was not above teasing, but looked on John as a son and wanted him happy. He normally didn't even consider relationships because of his condition, but his condition did not occur to him now.

One more set of stairs, the waterfall sounded more strong than loud. He climbed very slowly up this last set of stairs staring at the apparition waiting for him until finally he was at her level with nothing between them but perhaps twenty feet of space to go. She was looking at the waterfall but knew he approached. She had long brown hair, a light blue pleated top that perfectly matched dark blue jeans, and a red and black silk scarf. John stopped. He could not get any closer. You see beautiful people everywhere you go, and any billboard model, you might say, could take your breath away, but what John saw here was beauty from another dimension. He was no longer breathing.

"Hi John." He breathed like it was his first breath and he had never done it before. There just can't be any pretense with somebody that beautiful. Unless you are blind you are confessing worship. But John was getting something back. There was such emotion coming from her, a sly smile because she knew things he didn't know. Love and admiration, and a sad concern, these feeling emanated from her. The clues were falling in place and he wished they wouldn't. He was dreaming.

He took one more step toward her and suddenly everything he could see turned translucent. It was like another reality was trying to poke through this one.

"I wouldn't do that," she said. John shut his eyes, held his breath, and held up his hands in absolute surrender praying not to wake up. "Please not yet." John resigned himself.

When he opened his eyes he found himself locked in her gaze. He could not look away for a second. He had never been one to hold eye contact like this. He thought to himself, "I'm staring," but he was powerless. Did he dare speak? Her blue eyes effortlessly looked straight through to his soul.

The figure smiled, she glowed, and she was radiant. She put out her hands palms facing John and joined the tips of her thumbs together. She had made a frame in which she studied John as if she was composing a picture. She seemed pleased.

There was no telling how much time it took, but finally he could speak. "You know my name," he said. "What is your name?"

She gave him a sly look. John felt that if she never spoke another word, if they stood there frozen in time forever in that moment, it would be Heaven. He would be content. What in all of life could follow a moment with her?

"That is for you to find out." She paused, and then said, "For starters."

John let out a heavy sigh. "I'm dreaming. I know I'm dreaming. That is the only way you could be so beautiful." He paused in wonder after making such a statement. When he saw that she heard him he couldn't help but let a few tears slip. He prayed to God, or her, it didn't matter which, "Thank you for letting this last long enough for me to tell you how beautiful you are."

She wept too. "My John."

If this was going to last another second he had to ask. "Are you actually a creation of my dreams?"

Now she really did laugh and poke his pride, embarrassing him. "Silly you. You're not that good. Just maybe you have it backwards."

Then she got serious. "John, you are dreaming, yes, but I am not." She dropped her head and looked down, apparently at a loss for words. What words could follow what she had just said?

He stared at her, noticing the world was no longer translucent and feeling he could burn her image into his soul. He wished he could have some composure but this was too much. He spoke, "I don't want to be dreaming. I don't want to wake up and not see you again, and not get to know you. This seems even too good for dreaming, but you said I am." He fought back tears and lost.

She looked at him with such love. "John," she said. Then she looked at the waterfall for what seemed like a long time, but then looked back. Her eyes were such a perfect deep blue, and so soft and warm. She wore a necklace of dark blue beads and a matching bracelet. Her beauty almost hurt him. He just adored her and could not help what he was looking at. She looked at him in a way he had never been seen before. It was as if she would miss nothing. She lifted her hand as if tracing him with it.

"This is right," she said. "You will get to know me. You will learn where dreams can take you, and where they can't. Have some faith. John, I don't have all the answers either, not yet anyway, and not enough. Not enough." A tear slid down from the corner of her right eye. Seeing her in pain was turning the best dream he had ever known into a nightmare. What could be hurting her?

"Searching for each other is where our worlds join, and where our happiness can be found. Keep looking for me John. Please. I need you more than anything."

She put her hands up to her face as if in shock and sorrow as a little owl swooped their way. "I will," John promised quickly as he felt their time slip away. "I will."

The little owl landed on the window sill. The big old tom cat awoke instantly from the deepest of sleep. It leapt from the comfortable recliner where it had slept to the top of a bookcase, walked along the bookcase with its eyes glued to that owl, leapt down on John's bed, and scurried over to the window. The owl flew off. "I will," said John. "I will...kill you Sebastian." He plopped the cat on his chest. It purred loudly, as if claiming innocence of an unspeakable crime. But it just must have been time for that dream to end.

"Alright," John said to the cat. "You're a good cat. I guess I get to enjoy you for another day." Those were words John had been telling his cat every day for a long time. There was a reason he didn't take things for granted. But this morning he told Sebastian something more. The bed sheets were tucked very tightly. It took some time, but as he got up, petting the big cat on the head, he looked at it quite seriously and spoke. "Sebastian, there is somebody I really want you to meet. But I don't know her name."

2

Close Encounters

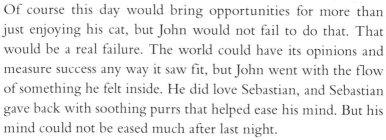

Of course this day would bring opportunities for more than just enjoying his cat, but John would not fail to do that. That would be a real failure. The world could have its opinions and measure success any way it saw fit, but John went with the flow of something he felt inside. He did love Sebastian, and Sebastian gave back with soothing purrs that helped ease his mind. But his mind could not be eased much after last night.

He was so thankful he did not have any cases pending. There was no way he could tear himself away from the thoughts racing through his mind. "Was that a dream?" He found it so merciful that there were no obligations to distract him from that dream. He had to relive it over and over and over again. He would never be the same. Dreams were his business and this was way over his head. He was suddenly part of a couple who needed to find each other. Reasoning failed him in every attempt to understand what had happened. How could he possibly find out her name? How could he ever find her? Did he have to dream? Was that the only way? How could she need him more than anything? Who is she? He was dreaming but she was not?

He had to stop the mental storm. Just listen to the purring. Scratch behind the ears and you have put that cat in Heaven even though it just tore you out of there.

"She is looking for me?" "I'm her John?" "Have some faith."
"Silly you." This was not going to stop any time soon, and John
had learned pretty well not to fight when you can't win. Looking
at her in that dream was the most incredible experience of his life.
He sighed. Dreams crash and burn all the time. That's what kept
him in business. Maybe it was his turn to live it. Was it possible
he might never see her again? Never figure out her name? But
then, "You will get to know me." This was all so powerful. He
was not just remembering. He was reliving, and that became
living. He felt embarrassed at being so pegged. This stranger had
come along and had his number, and boy she really did. "You're
not that good." What could he say? It was all the truth. He could
not have dreamed up such beauty in a million life times. He had
to love her. He already did. He had just found who he loved. But
he needed to find her again and there was no way to do that. She
had said, "You will get to know me." John would cling to that,
come what may.

"Ellen," her exasperated mother called to her through the
bathroom door. "You don't have to be a glamour model for a
babysitting job."

"I'll be right there, just a minute."

"I heard that five minutes ago. Susan is expecting us, she has
an appointment."

"Okay I'm ready, no wait, my eyes, just a minute more I
promise."

"Geez Ellen, I'm calling Susan and letting her know we're
leaving NOW."

Susan was pacing. She felt guilty for making a nail appointment,
but all her friends kept telling her to do something for herself.
There didn't seem to be much of anything for her in her life. How
long had it been? Not just for a nail appointment, for anything.
The phone rang and she grabbed it before the first ring ended.

"Susan, its Jennifer. We're just leaving. Ellen has been driving me crazy but we'll make it. I'm so sorry for running late."

Susan was grateful to hear the voice of a friend. It was good to talk to somebody, anybody.

"Thank you so much Jen, and thank Ellen for me. I'll see you soon." She hung up the phone. She felt bad to inconvenience such nice people, but she would pay Ellen well for babysitting. It really was nice to think of getting out. Maybe there could even be somebody she knew there. God that would be great.

"I don't know about you kids. Why do you have to get all made up for babysitting? Who do you think will be there? It is just Danny and Caitlin. You are babysitting." Jennifer felt like teasing her daughter over the delay, but she also felt uncomfortable about this. It was about to get worse.

"I don't know, maybe Steven will get home before Susan is finished." Ellen had wanted to answer her mother's question, but she immediately knew she had blown it big time.

"Oh my God Ellen." Jennifer could not even begin to hide her disgust, even her horror. "Ellen, do you have any idea what a dear sweet woman Susan Richards is? Do you have any idea how much her friendship means to me? I was so proud my daughter would help her to get out and do something nice for herself. Do you mean to sit there and tell me you are doing this for a possible chance to flirt with her husband?" Jennifer actually started to cry.

John sat at his desk and wrote out some notes. He wanted to record everything about last night's dream. With the dream business you can't afford to miss a single detail. He had learned that over the years. You never know what clue is going to make all the difference. He read over what he had written and shook his head. This was just incredible. This angelic vision had said, "Just maybe you have it backwards." Was that a clue?

John headed for the door to go out for a very long walk. He walked every chance he could get. He needed to for his health, and he needed to today to sort through all the thoughts and feelings that were storming through his head.

"Don't worry Sebastian, I'll be back and get your motor going. You have plenty of food and water. If you can catch that owl do it."

He stepped out into the fresh air. As much as he longed to be back in that dream it was very good to feel his physical body breathe and struggle over the steps. He had on his New Balance sneakers to take him the distance today, and he wanted to go far. He walked to the end of his block and crossed the street heading into town. He wanted to flow through some crowds today before heading out into the country. He loved to feel the contrast of community and solitude. The sun was not far up in the sky yet. It shined into John's face. He held up his right hand and blocked the sunshine for a moment. He felt as if he held the sun in that hand. He moved his hand back beside his head and looked at the sunlight he had caught. Life felt mysterious to him, especially now.

There was a health club in town, and a big billboard with one heck of a female model working out. It said, "A Perfect Body Is Waiting for You." John looked at it now with complete immunity. It was as if he was looking at a mail box or a trash can. This was supposed to be the best humanity had to offer of feminine beauty, but John just muttered three words under his breath.

"Not even close."

"I'm sorry Mom. I didn't mean anything bad by it. He's just such a hunk, and he flirts with me." Ellen was not helping her cause.

"I don't want to hear anymore. Susan deserves better than this shit." There was an awkward silence and Ellen had found enough sense to keep quiet now. She knew her mother was capable of talking that way, but she also knew her mother had to be pretty near breaking down before the pain came out like that.

There was a long awkward silence, but Jennifer finally spoke. "Nobody deserves a hunk more than Susan. She never asked for one, but Steven seemed to be a Godsend...at first. Steven adored her. He would never be caught dead disrespecting his wife. I don't know what the hell happens. I will never forget their wedding."

Jennifer was driving pretty fast. She was very sorry to be running late, and now sorrier for Susan than she had been already. Her thoughts drifted to that wedding. Probably every woman in the place was jealous of Susan. They were jealous because Steven was not just a hunk. They were jealous because he truly cared for Susan the way every woman dreams a husband should, and he was not afraid to show it. Jennifer remembered watching Steven at the head table like the wedding was yesterday. He looked at Susan like he was the luckiest man in the world. He picked up a fork and he started tapping his glass to bring his beloved for a kiss, and Susan knew it. Every woman at the wedding knew it. Jennifer remembered wanting to tell Susan how happy she was for her... when she came up for air. Jennifer almost wished she could trade places at that moment and live a dream.

Lost in day dream distractions Jennifer was going way too fast and oblivious to a red light just as John was crossing the street, plenty distracted himself.

"Mom," Ellen screamed at the top of her lungs when she realized what was happening.

"Look out," a man screamed at John and was able to physically grab him and pull him back enough so the car just grazed him. Jennifer and Ellen did not hear any thud, but it was enough of a hit to spin him and send him crashing through a trash receptacle. Maybe John had been protected. He discovered that he had closed his eyes and promptly opened them, finding himself in one piece. He lifted himself up on his elbows and looked at the car speeding off in the distance. It was pointless as could be perhaps, but he offered an admonition to the vanishing driver, "Don't dream and drive."

"Oh my God, I'm so sorry," Jennifer wept.

"Jesus Christ," Ellen blurted out, but it was forgivable. She suddenly just wanted to help her mother. She did love her mother.

"Mom its Okay, it's Okay. A man pulled him out of the way, he's alright. I saw him getting up. We need to help Susan and it's Okay. We didn't feel anything hit the car, I know he's Okay. I'm so sorry Mom. It's all my fault."

Jennifer finally spoke. "I pray you're right Ellen. I'm just sorry too. There's no excuse. I hope we make it through the day. Let's just help Susan."

John absolutely took his time getting back on his feet. He kept his eyes fixed on the car as it faded from view. He had a strange feeling about it, but also a familiar feeling. A small crowd had gathered after this near disaster. The man who had probably saved his life helped him slowly get to his feet. John's eyes stared at the car like he was in a trance.

The man spoke to John, trying to lighten the mood. "I bet you'll be saying Hail Mary's all day long after this one."

There was a long silence before John finally tore his eyes from the direction of the car and gazed into the eyes of his rescuer and spoke. "I believe her name was Jennifer."

3

The Business Card

It just seemed like it should not have been too much to ask. What should have been a simple mundane routine had shaken several lives to the core. It had become an ordeal from which people hoped to survive, but it had actually come to pass. Susan would get her nails done today.

It just so happened, as if God realized Susan needed a break, her dear old friend Peggy was getting her nails done too. Peggy gave Susan a hug like there was no tomorrow and Susan did not want it to end. She didn't give thought to how she was hug starved, but this helped more than it had a right to help.

"Susan Richards I can't believe it. God how long has it been? Why do we let so much time slip away?" Peggy was a sweetheart.

"Gosh I don't know," Susan replied. "I just know it is so good to see you. Thank God you were here today of all days."

"Well its Saturday honey. That will do it. Come here on a Saturday and you've found me." That should have been funny, but for Susan it was a cold hard slap in the face. Her sorrow was not the norm. Other people had good times together and did fun things. Peggy didn't have to battle a load of guilt every day just to get out of the house once in a while. Susan was trying to show herself a good time, but instead she was being shown that her time has not been good at all, that her sorrow was not Okay. Her life was not Okay and she has been trying very hard not to look at it. Susan burst into tears.

"Susan Susan," Peggy was so shocked at the tears. "Are you Okay?"

"I'm sorry," Susan spoke. "I just don't get out much and I guess I'm not good at it."

There was an older professional woman getting her hair done right next to where the nail tables were located in that salon. She was waiting under the hair dryer, trying to mind her own business, but an outburst of tears is hard to ignore. It is especially difficult to ignore suffering when you have a heart of gold and know something about healing. This was a nurse. She was older, but gave off a young spirit. There was a haunting beauty about her. She had beautiful blue eyes, long brown hair, wore a light blue pleated top with perfectly matching dark blue jeans. She had a beautiful necklace of dark blue beads and a matching bracelet. She also had a red and black silk scarf.

Susan seemed Okay, so the older woman sat back in her chair showing no notice of the two old friends, but paying great attention now.

Peggy spoke up. "Susan you seem so uptight. I know everybody was blown out of the water by your story book romance with Steven. Are you still together? I know we haven't seen each other in a long time, but you know I'm your friend. You can talk to me."

Susan was very much choked up, but she tried to speak as best she could. "Yes we're still together, but not like we were. He's never home. Honest to God it is just never. The kids keep asking me why and I don't know what to tell them. He's so successful. We don't want for anything except him. I'm supposed to believe this is all for us and I'm supporting our hero, but God we can do without all the money he says he's making with these endless hours of work. The kids are growing up, and I'm not growing at all, except tired. I feel old. This is not what I dreamed it would be."

The older woman had taken in everything Susan said. It was her mission to do that, and she had one mission left.

Peggy consoled Susan and they caught up on their friendship, remembered the old times, and lamented the drag of reality and the loss of hope that comes with time. They didn't notice the nurse at all anymore.

But as the nurse left, her appointment completed, she managed to slip a business card into Susan's purse.

A close call with a car like that might leave some people feeling thankful to be alive, or just very very lucky. John felt that way before the car. The grateful feeling of a close call also wears off for most people. John lived every moment in that awareness. He lived and breathed grace. It didn't preclude heartbreaking sorrow, or fear, but it made those realities less a factor to consider. He was a cancer survivor. He often pondered how that gave him an unfair advantage. He walked around with full awareness of how precious life is while everybody else was nearly blind. He could see what matters. He could see what is beautiful. It was a lonely awareness, but a full one.

Remission meant being given your mission again. But in John's case it gave him an unheard of mission. It was after chemotherapy that he began dreaming differently. At first he thought he was losing his mind. But his incredible nurse helped him see he was finding it. "Have some faith," she would say. John stopped like he had hit a wall. "Have some faith." Was that a coincidence? He had been so lost in thought he didn't even know where he was. He pictured that apparition as best he could. He could hear her voice. "Have some faith."

"Okay, I'll have me some faith." John often talked to himself. He also told himself he wouldn't mind if God listened in. That way he could be talking to himself and praying at the same time. How efficient. "Have some faith." He felt his life force get stronger. Here was a clue, and he really needed one. He actually had a medical appointment Monday and could pay way more attention to his nurse this time. She was already his confidant. She not only knew about his dreaming. She helped him discover what he could do with dreams. He had been taught what his dreams could do by someone who said, "Have some faith." Now he longed to be taught where they can take him, and where they can't, by someone who said, "Have some faith."

"Yep, I'll keep that appointment." He knew each day was gift enough, but he wanted Monday now, but there was plenty of today left. He would still have to decide when to turn around, and then there would be the whole walk back. He had had about enough but there was a little boy hammering something on a telephone pole up ahead and he got curious. A man approaching a boy causes concern these days, but John would be truly a good man and let life happen.

"Hey there young man, you look busy. What are you up to?"

"I lost my cat. About a week ago it disappeared. I hope it's Okay. I've walked up and down all the streets around here every day and I haven't seen him. He's not in the road so he should be Okay, but maybe somebody doesn't know he's mine."

"That certainly could be. So I see you've made a poster and have a great picture of your cat Whiskers." He read the poster and was very impressed. The poster was very well made. "I have a cat named Sebastian. What's your name?"

"Anthony. People call me Tony. Whiskers has a black collar with his name on it."

"I see that in the picture. Tony, may I shake your hand?"

"Sure."

John did not have explanations for what he did or how it works, but he knew touching people was like touching an antenna. It made some kind of connection which made certain perceptions possible, like dreams. John took the boy's hand and appreciated the chance to perceive Tony.

John held Tony's hand for just a moment, but it was enough for impressions to start flowing into his mind. "Tony I want to ask you a question." John started to feel uncomfortable, but he wanted to help. It should be the right thing to do. He put his hand on Tony's shoulder. It would be inconspicuous but continue the connection.

"Okay," said Tony.

"Who is Tommy?"

"Oh Tommy is my best friend. He loves Whiskers too. We've played together with Whickers all the time. I think Whiskers is his favorite cat."

John looked like he was gazing up to Heaven, but his eyes were shut. Pictures started to stream through his head. Tony and Tommy were best of friends. He could see them playing with Whiskers. Suddenly he experienced something else. It was like a day dream, but it was showing him what happened to Whiskers. John felt almost physical pain. He could help Tony, and he should help Tony, but people would be hurt.

"Tony, I think I know how you can get your cat back. I want you to listen to me carefully, and do exactly as I tell you. I want you to take this poster, and show it to Tommy's mother. Tell her your cat Whiskers has been missing since last Friday. Tony, there is a shed behind Tommy's house, and on the left side of the shed there is a milk box nobody ever uses or pays attention to. I want you to tell Tommy's mother that she should look in that milk box. Don't go near it without her. Let her look in the milk box. Okay, will you do that?"

"Sure if you think it will help get Whiskers back."

"I think it will Tony. It has been quite a pleasure meeting you. I hope to see you and Whiskers next time I come for a walk this way."

"I hope so too. That would mean I have Whiskers back."

John kept smiling until he was out of sight of Tony. "Life ain't fair." In his mind John could easily get on a mental soap box. People play winners and losers, and it just makes them lose so much more. They were two friends playing with a cat having a great time. He headed home. He remembered how much he was looking forward to his appointment Monday. He could tell his nurse anything, and that dream was too much to keep to himself. But then, for some reason, he got strong second thoughts. What could he possibly say about such a dream? He shouldn't talk about that dream. John fought with himself for some time. Should he ever say anything about that dream? It was an incredible personal experience, but it was pushing the limits of sanity. He needed to talk to his nurse. There was something about her he had not realized. There had to be some connection. He kept hearing the words, "Have some faith." He suddenly realized these medical appointments can bring terrible news, or the worst. And he wasn't ashamed to admit he dreaded the bone marrow tests. He would most likely get another one of those. But when he thought about that dream he wondered if death was the way to "what's her name?" He spoke out to her like it was prayer. "You hear that what's her name? Can I speak your name and still live? I'm going to find out your name, maybe soon. Then I'll need your number."

Tony carried the poster toward Tommy's house. He checked out the shed in the back and saw the milk box just like the man said. That was weird. He wouldn't touch it. Tommy's Mom had to do that.

Tony knocked on the door.

"Tony, what brings you here? I'll get Tommy." Tommy's mother was very friendly.

"A man I met told me to come here to show you a poster I made. My cat Whiskers has been missing since last Friday and he said to show you the poster."

Tommy's mother looked at the poster and turned white as a ghost.

"Oh no," she said. "Tommy," she called out. "Tony is here and we have to talk about the cat you found."

"Tony," Tommy's mother spoke very seriously, "Who told you to come here? What else did he say?" She was very shaken up. It was bad enough to discover what her son had done, but someone had witnessed it. Someone knew about this. He must have been watching Tommy.

"It was just a nice man going for a walk. He might come back some time. He said to tell you to look in the milk box by your shed in the back yard. Tommy found a cat?"

Tommy came to the front door crying, and holding Whiskers. He couldn't look Tony in the face, but he did talk. "I'm sorry; I just wanted Whiskers with me for a while."

"You took my cat?" Tony was baffled but just wanted his cat back. "Whiskers I've missed you. I'm so glad you're alright." Tony hugged his cat. He wanted to be just a little boy who loved his cat. He did not want to deal with betrayal and forgiveness. Those things signal losing childhood. He could not think about Tommy right now.

"I want to see what is in the milk box." Tommy's mother tried to stay calm, but it wasn't working. "What else did that man tell you?"

"He just said it was a pleasure to meet me and he hoped to see me and Whiskers when he walked this way again. Now he can because I've got Whiskers back."

Tony carried Whiskers and followed Tommy's mother to the milk box. Tommy didn't want to come. Tommy's mother was as upset as she could be about what Tommy had done, and that some strange man out there seemed to know all about it. How could that be? They stopped at the milk box. "Okay," she said, "Let's see what this is about." She opened the milk box, gave a sigh of shock, and held her hands over her face. Inside the box there was a black cat collar with the name "Whiskers."

Later that night, much later, with the kids in bed and Steven not home yet, Susan tried calling his office. She got the machine again. "Where are you?" She kept calling that machine. She wanted to hear his voice, and that was the only way to do it. "Steven where are you? Why don't you answer me?" The tears flowed again and she slammed her purse down on the bed. The contents spilled, and there was the business card the nurse had slipped inside. She didn't recognize it and picked it up. She put on her reading glasses and brought it over to the light. A frightened look came over her face as she read the words across the card. "Broken Dreams Repaired." There was the name John Dreamer and a phone number. She put the card back in her purse, for now.

4

Fusheeswa

When Monday came John woke up with not just a headache, the headache. He put his hands over his face and rose groaning. As usual it took a while to work his way out of his tightly tucked sheets. He sat up, and after some time peeked through two fingers at Sebastian. The cat was curled at the foot of his bed purring full throttle.

"Good morning Mr. Motor. I guess I get to enjoy you for another day." John pet Sebastian on the head and scratched behind his ears. The cat soaked it up like he had paradise in his pocket. John was startled to notice something he had not seen. The red light on his answering machine was blinking. There was a message and he had missed it. He hit play.

"Hi John. This is Helen from Bayside Medical Center calling to remind you of your appointment with Dr. Bernard this coming Monday afternoon at 2PM. I'm looking forward to seeing my John. John, I gave out a business card today. There was a lovely woman in the hair and nail salon, but she is really hurting. I know it may be a few weeks, but this woman should call. See you at 2PM on Monday. Any problems just give us a call and we'll reschedule. Don't forget to fast."

He wanted to replay the message but the pain blanked out everything. He put his hands over his eyes and turned around.

It made him worse than dizzy. He just made it to the bathroom. He vomited with such intense heaves he thought he would not have organs left in his body. Flash backs of his dream flashed like fireworks through his head as he felt himself in death throws. He couldn't see through the flood of tears and vomit splashing all over the room, until finally it stopped. He clung to the bowl and just breathed. It had never felt so good to be breathing. Still breathing.

He spoke softly in prayer to his beloved dream girl. "I'm afraid you can't need me more than anything. What's left of me is not much to offer a goddess like you. I'm sorry I dreamed you, if that's what I did. Just know this, whatever is left of me for all time will be loving you." He lay down on his bathroom carpet and slept.

When he woke up the headache was less severe. He took it very slow getting up. From what he could guess looking at his clock he had been out for about three hours. There was still plenty of time to make his appointment. Maybe he would live. He did listen to the message, several times. The voice did sound like an older version of what's her name? It did say, "Hi John," and "My John." He didn't know what to tell Helen. He didn't know if he would live long enough to tell her anything. Time did lift the feelings of pain and sickness from his body. He thought about how he was supposed to fast before his appointment.

"If they want me on "Empty" that's sure what they'll get."

It was some distance from his house to Bayside, but he didn't want to drive when he felt this likely to drop dead at any moment. He decided to call a cab, but when he let his neighbor Joe know he had a medical appointment and to check on Sebastian if he didn't get home, Joe insisted on driving him.

"And don't worry about the cat. Sebastian and I are old friends." Joe had watched Sebastian before, sometimes for weeks at a time.

Joe gave John a pep talk as he was dropping him off at the

hospital. "You just give me a call for your pick up. You'll be fine, and if you don't believe me you're full of it."

John gave a thankful smile and wave- but he thought to himself, "That's what I'm afraid of."

"Here goes," John said to himself as he walked in the doctor's office where Dr. Gary Bernard, the head of the Oncology department himself would check him out. John was a difficult case, and over the years Helen saw to it that the best doctors at Bayside were doing all they could. A wave of nausea swept over him again and his headache was getting worse as well. He was in the right place.

"Well well, my John has"…Helen's voice slowed down when she got a good look at him, "returned. Good lord John you have had better days. Did you bring a suit case?"

John looked at Helen like the only family he had. When he was with her it was like coming home, but his strength was failing fast. He also saw she had a necklace of dark blue beads and a matching bracelet. It looked like the ones his dream girl had worn. He saw on the wall Helen's coat with a red and black silk scarf. He fainted.

He woke up in a hospital bed hooked up to IVs with Helen hovering over him.

"Alright young man, you have my attention. John we've run tests and I've mixed this special potion for you. I've got to tell you I've also been saying some prayers. You are some case. I think we need to get you dreaming big time."

"Helen, it's so good to see you too. Oh Helen, I feel terrible."

"I'm sure you do."

"Helen, I've got to talk to you. I need to know something."

"Well what's so important?"

"Helen, I had another dream. I think it had something to do with you."

"John I don't like the sound of this. Now you need to get some real rest."

"Helen if I die tonight I need to know something."

"What is it John?" Helen was usually the pillar of strength but John's dreaming could make her very nervous.

"Helen do you have any family? Have you ever been married or had children?" John and Helen had been very close for years, but personal questions like this had just never come up. Helen couldn't hide her shock. Her face even betrayed horror. John had never seen Helen so visibly shaken and he never saw that coming.

"John, there are some things that belong in the past. I'm a private person and with all due respect what's past is past."

"Helen I would never, ever want to hurt you."

"Then stop asking questions John. You need to sleep, drop it."

John was having the worst day of his life. For all he knew it might be his last and he was hurting the person he needed most. He couldn't believe he had been so abrupt with Helen, but he was driven over his dream. He took Helen's hand, kissed it, and looked deep in her eyes before passing out.

"Good night John and sweet dreams." But John would not have a sweet dream. Helen had not been this shaken up for a long long time. It had taken decades to bury all her pain. Of course John might mean well, but wherever he was going with this dream he better turn around. Helen checked on John over and over again. This was one amazing patient she had, and she couldn't bear the thought of losing him. But John was very sick. Often as she sat by his side she put her hand on his shoulder and rubbed him gently hoping to sooth his pain. Helen knew some things John could do with his dreams, but she did not know the power of touch to serve as an antenna.

"My John," she said gently stroking his cheeks, rubbing his shoulder, holding his hand. She ran her fingers through his hair. "Dam I'm good," she thought to herself. One of the things she hoped to accomplish in her experimentation with the intravenous medicines was to help patients retain their hair when receiving chemotherapy. She cared very much about giving people dignity.

In John's case she had struggled very hard over experimental medications when the traditional chemotherapy drugs were not helping him. She could not have imagined the side effects the medications would have on John, side effects that would make them both question reality. It was after an early session of chemotherapy during which Helen adjusted the intravenous solution with her own created medication, desperate to help this special man, that John started having his vivid powerful dreams. What was even more incredible was that he became able to stand on the bridge between his dreaming and waking states, and carry others across that bridge to find what they needed on the other side. Mostly, it was a walk through memories. John could help people relive what may have seemed like their worst nightmare, but with more clarity another view can be possible.

Helen shook her head looking at her poor sick John, lying there so helpless. She hoped and prayed she could help him. She always gave her best. All her nursing awards just seemed like a distraction. Meetings and dinners just took away from time caring for patients, and a patient well again was more thanks than she could properly take in. She did pray for John as she tended him, taking vital signs, watching the IV drip. It was all so unfair. Illness always seems that way, but somehow with John Helen felt worse about it. Poor John was like a yoyo back and forth between remission and his death bed, and Helen held the string. Each time she wondered if it would be the last.

"Fusheeswa," Helen thought to herself as she looked at her IV potion. It was such a magic word. Helen remembered when she was a little girl sick in bed with an awful fever. A lot of people seemed pretty scared, but not her mother. She remembered Mom coming in to her bedroom. I've got a real special medicine for you now honey. I made it myself." Helen's mother had such love and faith. It was always an inspiration to remember anything about her mother.

"What is it Mommy?" Helen asked.

25

"This is all my love for you, all mixed in to a special pill."

"What's it called?" Helen always needed to know everything. Her mother smiled in surprise.

"Oh, I wasn't expecting that. Let's see…it is called," Helen's mother gave her that magic smile, "Fusheeswa. It is all the medicine you'll ever need. It can beat anything." Fusheeswa would pull Helen through a lot of times over the years.

Helen looked at her watch and adjusted John's IV drip. "Hope my Fusheeswa does the trick," Helen thought to herself. She put her hand back on John's shoulder. Her constant loving strokes served as the perfect antenna. It made the connection.

5

Finding The Name

John began to dream. He stood in the emergency room as a woman was frantically carried in on a stretcher. Paramedics were all over her, a man trying to get through calling her name over and over, "Helen, Helen." It was Helen, twenty years old, in labor.

"You've got to help her," the man screamed. Doctors, nurses, paramedics, it was pure chaos. Something was very very wrong, but John couldn't see what. He didn't move his feet but followed as Helen was wheeled in to surgery.

"Get every best surgeon in this hospital in here now," one doctor demanded with authority to get what he wanted, "We're saving this baby."

John could not believe his eyes as this young Helen suffered through such a terrible ordeal. Doctors yelled back and forth, all kinds of IVs were set up. Vital signs were called out over and over. It was absolutely touch and go for what at least seemed like hours. There was some strange man watching all this with John, but he couldn't get a good look at him. There was something desperate about him. For all the fear John was feeling over this young Helen, he feared that stranger more.

The baby was saved, but not Helen. John saw the nurses wrap the baby in a pink blanket and carry it off to maternity, but Helen was in trouble. John seemed glued to the floor, off to the side somewhere, but he could tell what was going on. He heard somebody yell, "Clear." This couldn't be happening but there was nothing John could do but watch, and then wait.

"Good bye Helen." The stranger slipped away. John yelled out pointing at him as he left, "Who is that man? What is he doing? Somebody watch him." John felt terrified, but he realized he was dreaming. Nobody heard him. He wasn't there.

It seemed like another day. Nurses kept drawing blood, changing IVs, taking blood pressure, Helen would not wake up. As hours passed on during whatever day this was the authoritative doctor sat by her side. He spoke, "The world needs more nursing students like you, acing your biochemistry, getting everyone in the internship program talking. I couldn't be more proud. But I told you having a baby would kill you, you had to try to prove me wrong?"

It was a very uncomfortable dream. John was in that rare state he could sometimes achieve. He knew he was dreaming, but not dreaming. He was watching Helen's past. His rapport with Helen was deep. They were connected. No one came to see Helen but doctors and nurses. This went on for days, then weeks. Helen lay in a coma and John could only stand by and watch her sleep there day and night. He had no idea how much time was going by. All of a sudden all sorts of people came to look in on Helen, doctors and nurses, and then policemen and men in suits looking very serious and asking all kinds of questions of everybody and taking notes. Finally all the care she had received paid off, Helen woke up.

"Where's my baby?" They were the first words out of her mouth. John felt the weight of the world's horror as they became the second words, the third words, and it did not stop. All the people around her looked at each other. They had been dreading hearing this question. There was no answer. Nobody could answer that question. This is not possible. Nobody had the answer, not doctors, nurses, detectives, lawyers, or even the FBI. There was no baby. But John had seen it. That stranger. John had never seen his face.

Helen screamed like there would be no tomorrow, or if there was she would refuse it. John yelled out her name as loud as he could. "Helen, Helen," then he woke up.

"You don't have to yell I'm right here." Helen's soothing voice, like that of an angel, made him feel lighter. Then he noticed he felt rather good. He looked at Helen with unrestrained love, and unrestrained tears.

"John I have some good news, and some bad news. The good news is you look like a million bucks. Your vital signs are back up where they should be."

"What's the bad news?" John dared to ask.

"The bad news is…it has been a week."

Whatever reality Helen was talking about it did not compare to the one he had just taken in. His intense gaze into Helen's soul told her he knew. Somehow he knew.

John spoke softly, but not from weakness. He loved Helen like his own mother. He would never set out to hurt her, but the truth must come out.

"Helen, Helen, I'm so sorry. I don't know what this is all about, but it is about something. It is about you, and me, about dreams, and about your baby."

Helen broke into tears. "No John I can't."

"Helen," John gazed at her in a way that communicated his life depending on this. His dream had him completely locked in a mission.

"You've seen miracles; you've helped me do what can't be done to save what can't be saved, you've seen it. Maybe we have the same dream. Helen, did you have a name picked out? I need to know her name."

Helen was a broken woman sitting there frozen in time. A fountain of tears flowed from her eyes, staining her clothes, making a puddle on the floor. This was over forty years of tears coming out in an afternoon.

"John, it was forty two years ago. I was young and foolish, too much in love. It was my dream to be the perfect wife and mother. I like to hope maybe I'm a better nurse because I've been there and know all too well the frailty of human beings and their dreams. I can't ever know what it was all about. I've asked myself a million times what went wrong, where she could be, if she is even alive, why this had to happen."

John spoke up, "Helen, one thing we so seldom seem to know is why. But we just follow our hearts and do what we feel is best. You always do that Helen. Now I have had this most incredible dream. I don't have answers, but I sure have questions. I need to follow my heart Helen. I'm feeling the lady in my dream was your daughter, is your daughter. She wants me to find her. She knew my name, God knows how Helen. When I asked her to tell me her name she told me it was for me to find out. I didn't have a clue in the world how I could possibly ever find out that precious name. Now I'm betting you can just tell me."

Helen took John's hand in hers. Tears streamed down her face. She gazed downward for a while. John thought of how the dream lady looked away at the falls after telling him that he was dreaming, but she was not. He looked deeply in Helen's eyes. Only in that dream had he ever looked in someone's eyes like this before. The same enchanting love lingered in that moment, however long it was.

It was so difficult for Helen to say it, a secret kept locked in a broken heart for forty two years.

"We had a name picked out. One of my prayers is that she was given that name."

"She was Helen." John was able to give Helen that truth. It didn't compare with what Helen gave John.

"Kari."

6

A Broken Dream

The next two weeks were uneventful. John was feeling young and spry, like a teenager. His special dreams often gave him rejuvenation. In spite of how many times this happened Helen was never prepared for the new John. He had given her quite a scare with his health, but perhaps a greater scare with his dream. He never wanted to hurt her. He had to wonder if he could help.

It was a mixed blessing to be back to some kind of routine. John walked each day, pondered the dreams, of Helen and Kari. Sometimes he prayed. It was a prayer to speak that name, "Kari." He felt Helen's pain. How could it be going through life wondering about a daughter you never knew? How could he find her? What would happen if he did?

On one of his walks he actually saw Tony and Tommy playing with Whiskers.

"Well," he thought. "Kids are better at getting past these indiscretions than adults. Isn't it better to be friends?" John whispered, "Thanks," to a close friend in the sky.

He noticed the walks did feel lonely. They never had before. He wished he was walking with Kari, hand in hand. He was all about making dreams come true for others. "How about one for me?" John got a chill. "Okay, let's not get selfish." But walking hour after hour did get lonely. It was a special kind of pain.

He took it as a kind of gift. It is good to love somebody, even if it hurts. He walked along a row of stores and some pictures caught his eye. It was a camera store, and all across the big front window were pictures of the planets taken by NASA probes. He thought about finding Kari. He looked at the stark barren image of Mercury, the bright somewhat fuzzy image of cloud covered Venus, the orange desolate Mars with haunting ice caps. Then he stared at the beautiful blue sphere of Earth. He put his finger up to the glass. "I'll look there."

That evening, back at his home the phone rang. John looked at the clock, 8PM. He picked it up.

"Hello."

"Hello, is this John?"

"Yes."

"My name is Susan." There was a silence, a familiar silence. This was always difficult for everyone. There is so much pain in the world, and it is even painful to ask for help. "Somehow your business card got in my purse."

"Susan," there was a soothing warmth to his voice. "Susan I know how that card got there. Someone thought you were very special. Someone cared about you and wanted to help you with a broken dream. I may be able to help. I will be able to try."

It was decided John would visit Susan at 7PM at her house Saturday night. She would have had trouble finding a babysitter, and she could count on her husband to be missing in action. It was strange for the first time in her life to be glad he was out. She was coming to realize her lack of contact with the outside world was very bad for her. The blessing of one day out getting her nails done had taught her more than she wanted to know. But she needed to learn.

That Friday John spent the day getting himself psyched for another case. It had been some time since he had been working. He needed to get organized. Dreaming, and following trains of thought could take John far outside of himself. He needed notes to keep him grounded. At different times through his days he would write everything down. Thoughts and feelings that he may not understand might mean something later when he least expected it. He wrote down all he could remember of his dreams. Everything he could relive about being with Kari, everything he could remember about Kari's birth. Living without ever knowing her mother could be the source of great pain. Was that why she cried? That pain could be terrible.

It was difficult for John to deal with having his own dream, wanting with all his heart to find Kari, and yet he seemed to have another broken dream calling him. It would be difficult to concentrate on somebody else's problems. He had to pray, and could only take on faith that he better help this Susan now.

Saturday finally came. She heard the knocking at the door and her heart skipped a beat. This was no whim. Susan had been hurting for so long it had created desperation. Life was too painful to endure this way day after day. She didn't care about herself anymore, but she cared about her kids. She kept a can of mace spray in her pocket just in case.

"Hi Susan," the handsome man with the soothing voice and disarming smile could only be John. He held out his hand and took hers for a moment. It was tricky, and he hoped it would be enough. He felt the warmth of her hand. She was shy, but smiled and felt comfortable. There was much emotion in her face, and obvious innocence. She was very beautiful.

"Hi John, come on in. The kids are upstairs watching a DVD. Would you like anything? Some tea?"

"How did you know?" John smiled. The two were connecting well.

"You must think I'm the most desperate woman on earth." Susan spoke faintly, ashamed to feel so week.

"No, that is who I'm looking for but I don't think it's you." John immediately realized what he had said was so out of focus.

He may be so distracted with Kari he would not be able to work a case. Susan's dream had to become his life if he was to help her. He had to get a grip. This moment taught him how much he had been consumed with his own growing dream. He had to let it go.

John spoke, "I'm sorry Susan. I briefly lost my train of thought." John spoke very slowly. "I know this has been so difficult for you, and you must have so many questions, fears and such concerns. Please be assured we will take our time. We will talk, we will learn from each other, and no decisions will be made until you are fully comfortable."

"I've never done anything so crazy in my life. I'm an intelligent woman. I'm curious; I can't believe you have a business card like that, but..." Susan started weeping, "I need you to be for real."

Here was the chance, John took it. He held Susan in his arms, connecting. As frightened and broken as Susan felt, it was comfortable to be in a man's arms again. It brought back memories of how things should be. It was a reminder of her dream.

John had a large note pad and started taking notes. "It helps me clarify my thoughts," John explained. He asked Susan about the people in her life. Who was she close to? Who was family to her? He had written eight names on his pad. Susan named seven. Susan mentioned her husband Steven, her son Danny, and her daughter Caitlin.

She also mentioned Jennifer and Peggy. She spoke of her parents, but they lived far away and there had been very few visits over the years. John looked at the name Barbara written on his pad but didn't say anything.

"I'd like to meet the kids if you don't mind."

"Well Okay. I didn't expect that, but they're still up. Danny, Caitlin, please come down here for a minute." John won them over in an instant with his smile, and his very long handshakes.

"You have beautiful children Susan. So tell me about Steven."

Susan poured her heart out for about an hour. She shared photos from some of her many photo albums. She was very particular about photo albums. They were all well put together and labeled with dates and places. John was very impressed with these artistic creations. Susan had put these together with such loving care. Gold lettering told of "Dating," "Vacations," and "Caitlin's First Birthday." Pictures of people's lives were a treasure. A precious treasure indeed. Thinking about it made it seem strange that people did not take such care of their photos. John wished he had pictures of his life like this. He wrote in his notes about this strong feeling of photos.

Steven was a handsome looking catch. He also clearly loved his family. He looked like he was in heaven at an amusement park with Danny and Caitlin in his arms, both at once. Caitlin was just an infant in the pictures, but not left behind. Susan started to tear up looking at their better times. She thanked John for letting her share the albums. He had only looked at a few of them, but the sharing and caring meant a lot to Susan. She had not had anyone pay such attention to her for a long time. It brought back more memories of how Steven used to be. She kept apologizing for taking up so much of John's time. John gave her loving looks of discipline which just invited her to go deeper. She was a beautiful woman with a precious heart. When he noticed her beauty and felt for her dream he could hear Kari's voice in his head, "Have some faith." He had spoken it out loud.

It was John's turn to speak. "Susan, first of all thank you for inviting me into your home, into your heart, and into your dream. Peggy and Jennifer and others you mentioned sound like angels all praying for you. That will help our cause. It is a very personal thing for us to work together on your dream. You have been as honest as can be with me, and I'll always be honest with you. There are no guarantees. I will not keep your money, other than my expenses, unless we both feel your dream is back intact. If we can get there- then nothing you could pay me would ever be enough. That's when I like to discuss fees, John smirked. Susan was a very good woman. She was a sad woman, but now she had someone on her side. She had someone at least trying to help.

John smirked again, "So Steven is in real estate. I guess I have to buy a house."

"Susan got a look of horror." John put up his hand.

"Relax, I'll just look. You can trust me Susan." He had a soothing way about him that made Susan wonder if he might be an angel. She needed one badly enough to buy it. She agreed to John's terms, to work with him in any way she could. She was putting her life in his hands, but she felt that she should. His light touch with a sense of humor seemed to make this whole impossible situation possible. Susan was afraid to hope, but with the love in John's eyes she couldn't help it. It felt good.

As he was leaving John held out his hand. Susan took it. They stood there for a long time.

"Thank you so much for coming," Susan meant those words with all her heart.

"You won't need the mace," John winked at her. "Talk to you soon."

7

The Richard's Case

Back at home, with Sebastian fed, John spread out his papers on the table. He created what looked like a medical chart for Susan Richards. He poured over the notes he had taken and pondered what could have happened to such a perfect couple and such a beautiful dream. It seemed anyone with any sense would love Susan. She was a real sweetie. Steven was very lucky, but maybe not if he couldn't see it. He must have had something right about him to choose Susan, and to be chosen by her. Their children were adorable. Danny was six years old, Caitlin was four. They deeply missed their father. That pushed John's buttons. He must not go into this judgmentally, but the kids were the victims here as much as Susan.

Susan had told John that about a year and a half ago there was one night when Steven did not come home. It had been the worst night of Susan's life, fearing for his safety and wondering where he could be. He called the next morning to say he had fallen asleep at the office after working so hard on some mortgage forms for a client. Susan had called the office many times. Why didn't that wake him? He did rush home and was as apologetic as could be, but something was wrong- and stayed wrong. Steven seemed very defensive, very fearful, and worst of all distant. He absolutely denied an affair, and their incredible passion up until that one day was proof enough he could not have been anything but fully in love with Susan.

The photo albums especially haunted him. He was so impressed at the care that had gone in to putting them together so tastefully. Most families even if they have special times don't capture them this well. This family had had lots of wonderful times for being so young. They were just getting started, but did know what they had, did capture every precious moment, and did treat each single picture as a treasure to be especially displayed. It was such a testament to a beautiful dream being lived out as few of them are.

Some kind of affair would be the most common suspicion. But affairs happen after dreams are broken. In spite of how uncomfortable it was to discuss with a stranger, Susan had revealed how incredible their passion had been even up to the night before Steven didn't come home. It didn't add up.

"So what happened?" John looked at Sebastian as if expecting an answer, and then smirked. He was very moved by his evening with Susan and her children, and really hoped he could help.

On the following Monday John called Bayside Hospital and arranged to meet with Helen that afternoon. He did need to discuss recent blood test results, the Susan Richards case he was working on, and if possible…finding Kari. He wasn't feeling as wonderful as he had been but still walked to the hospital with a spring in his step. It would be good to see Helen.

As John was walking through the hospital entrance way he looked back out and saw Susan Richards running in to the hospital with a look of panic on her face.

"Susan what's wrong?" He caught her attention.

"Oh John, Danny's bus was in an accident, he's been taken here."

John was shocked and needed to comfort Susan. "We'll find him, I'm sure he's alright, will we meet Steven?"

"Steven said to keep him posted." Susan wiped a tear from her eye but was in too much of a panic to see how that struck John, but he did have to catch his breath. As they hurried through the hospital looking for the Emergency Room and Danny they passed a large picture of a rainbow along a wall. John thought Steven not being there was like someone had stolen a color from the rainbow. It just shouldn't be. This belonged in a bad dream, but it was real.

They found Danny in the ER. His left elbow had been bruised pretty badly, but he would be fine. The school had insisted everyone on the bus get a thorough medical exam. Danny was so glad to see Mom. An attending nurse asked John if he was Danny's father. "Oh, I'm just a friend of the family here for my own appointment." John had even forgotten that until the question.

"I am so glad you're Okay," John said to Danny. "That must have been quite an accident. You'll have quite a story to tell Dad."

"By the time I see Dad I'll forget it." The words hung in the air between John and Susan and John felt like he had to push them away to move. He put his arm on Susan's shoulder. All he could do was tell her, "I'll do my best."

"So tell me about the accident," John was very concerned about this special boy.

Danny was not used to attention, and he lit up like a Christmas tree.

"It was real cool, the wheel fell right off the bus. We skidded into a telephone pole."

"Holy cow," John exclaimed. Danny could tell John was impressed. It made him feel proud.

"Which wheel came off?" John asked.

"The right rear wheel. I don't know why a wheel would fall off."

"Neither do I," John said- and he wrote this information down in his notebook.

"Every detail," John whispered to himself.

"Well, I've got to get to my own appointment. I'm so glad you're alright Danny. I hope to see you again soon."

"Me too," Danny beamed. Susan got a pained look on her face. It was bitter sweet, but so good to see Danny bask in a man's attention.

"There's my John." Helen's voice charmed him every time. He did notice that she seemed a little tired. She was an awesome nurse and had probably sacrificed sleep for somebody.

"How have you been feeling?" Helen asked him.

"I've been feeling like any man with the world's greatest nurse working his case." John blew the words like kisses in her face. "And you have the best potions." John knew Helen did something with his IVs but he vowed never to ask.

"You're sure you've been feeling fine?" John began to realize Helen had some concern.

"Yes, I'm feeling like my old self. Is something wrong?"

"We need another blood sample. I hope there's nothing wrong, but there seem to be some new anomalies. A good sample should clear everything up." Helen could not bring herself to tell John what the test results seemed to indicate. She had never held back before. She managed to convince herself the previous tests just had to have been flawed. It would be wrong to get John worried without more conclusive proof.

John went to another area of the hospital where several vials of blood were taken. A senior member of the hospital staff seemed to be interested in John's condition. John read his identification badge, "Dr. Tom Brady." There were no words spoken between the two, no introductions. Dr. Brady just nodded at John as if he knew something, but there was no telling what. John returned to Helen's office to continue their visit.

"Will you be needing more of my potion?" Helen did seem to be able to read his mind at times. It was an incredible secret between them.

John let Helen know it would be some time before he would be ready to attempt a dream repair, but he was working on the case now. John looked at Helen and took a deep breath. Dreams were a secret they shared, but Kari was a secret Helen wanted to keep. John had been wondering where to begin for weeks.

"Helen, my dream about Kari was the most incredible experience of my life. You are the one person on this planet who could even begin to understand."

Helen had had some time to ponder John's mention of her baby and his need to learn her name. A healing process had begun. She now had enough strength to speak about it.

"Well maybe Kari can understand it too." John gave up trying to hold his composure. Helen hugged him like a mother should, for a long time.

John looked at this incredible lady through his tears and said, "You are way too sweet to be a mother-in-law." Helen got the joke, and tears and laughter began to release the sad tension that had haunted both of them.

Helen could dish it back. "I prayed I was saving your butt for something special, but that would beat all." Helen got serious. "John for all these years I've fought with myself every night, fighting to believe that it was real, that it was not some nightmare I was making up in my head. I've been missing my baby for all these years. I guess I spent the first thirty years looking for her, but I had to give up. These last twelve I've just lit a candle now and then and said my prayers, hoping she's alright out there somewhere."

"John I can't bear the thought of you spending all the time I have over Kari. I don't know if she's alive. I never got to see her," Helen cried. "She could be on the other side of the planet."

John and Helen sat in silence looking at each other, and then they both said the exact same thing at the exact same time. "Have some faith."

8

Real Estate

"Steven Richard's office, Barbara speaking, may I help you?" John felt his hand crushing the phone receiver. He looked at his hand and eased up the grip.

"Hi my name is John and I'd like to make an appointment with Steven to discuss renting with possible option to buy."

The appointment was set for Thursday at 5PM. 5PM, John wanted to go with whatever he was told, but a person should be leaving work at that time to go home to their family. John wrote his notes in Susan Richard's chart. Whatever else Barbara might be she was certainly a key figure in Steven's life, right there with him all the time. It was easy for John to expect the worst, but he could never expect the worst from people. He would be more shocked than he could imagine.

At 5PM on Thursday John walked through the office doors of Richard's Realty. The woman who greeted him looked somehow more like a picture than a real woman, or perhaps a walking mannequin. "You must be John, right on time. I like that. I'm Barbara we spoke on the phone. John Dreamer, I guess we'll have to find your dream house." John felt like he was meeting the performance of a woman, a very creepy feeling. He responded.

"Yes, I'm John. Great directions." John wondered why he had said that. It was phony and just not something he would ever say.

He offered Barbara his hand. The moment they touched he got such a chill he let go in shock. He smiled hoping to conceal that blunder but also realizing he had blown a major opportunity for connection. He had to focus. His sensitivity was working over time.

Barbara spoke as she led John to Steven's office. "Steven's office is right this way."

They approached close enough for Steven to hear what was said. "I'm Steven's administrative assistant. You can probably figure out I'm the brains of the business and I'm happy to be taking care of Steven." John couldn't wait to start writing his notes, and they wouldn't have anything to do with real estate.

"Hi, Steven Richards, thank you for coming." John gave Steven a decent hand shake. Steven had heard Barbara's comments but couldn't respond. John felt his fear and knew he was following a script. Somehow Barbara owned him and John could hardly shake the chills. He thought about his cancer but realized this chill was something even worse, but it was not coming from inside him.

Steven tried to be upbeat, "So how can we help you today?"

"I'm looking to rent or buy a place closer to Bayside Medical Center from where I live now." John looked about the room and asked a strange question. "So is this your office?"

"Yes, of course." Steven replied.

John felt strength in being the one without fear. He would operate from strength. He looked in Steven's eyes and spoke. "Steven I know your wife Susan, and your son Danny. I met them at Bayside Medical Center Monday after the school bus accident. So I'm wondering with such a beautiful wife and son why you have no family pictures in your office."

Steven looked pathetic but Barbara leaped in for a rescue attempt. "Oh it was my idea to clean up the office. He did have pictures everywhere, but that was distracting from business. We have to stay focused to deliver the best customer service, and that's what we do. So you want to be closer to Bayside, I hope it's not for medical care at that dump." John didn't even flinch. Bayside needed no defense. But he could feel Steven's embarrassment.

John did want to stir the pot and learn more about what he was facing. He spoke up, but only from that task. "Bayside is where the school sent Steven's son. Did they take good care of Danny?" John did want to know how that special boy was doing. He was probably doing better than his Dad.

Steven spoke, but weakly, "Danny is much better. Just an elbow bruise. The care was alright I suppose."

John struck again, "Which hospital was Danny born in?"

Barbara jumped in to save Steven again. She snapped, "Oh it has only been the past year Bayside has gone downhill. Anyway we need to talk about houses. Steven show John the townhouse listings, and don't forget to ask the questions."

John felt like he was living in some nightmare. He wanted to be anywhere but in that office. But he did feel some hope. Steven did not love Barbara, nobody could. The question was what she had on him. Then a thought flashed in John's mind that did make him flinch. "Maybe it was just what Steven thought she had."

Steven asked questions, "Will it just be you? Do you have any pets?"

"Just me and my cat," John answered feeling slightly better. He was on the case, and learning things.

"Fowl things," Barbara muttered. John looked in Steven's eyes. It was like looking from a garden paradise into a prison cell. How did Steven get there, and could John get him out?

Barbara spoke up, somehow gleeful, "Tomorrow is Friday. We can show the townhouses at 3PM, and several single family homes near Bayside. Then we can grab a bite to eat. On us John, does that work for you?"

"Sure." John looked very pleased, but it was because he would get the hell out of there and breathe. He shook hands with Steven, as long as possible. Then he turned to give Barbara a proper goodbye. He held out his hand.

"Nice grip," Barbara spoke seductively, "Like Steven's."

John took a long shower when he got home, followed by hours of writing his notes.

Human relationships, "Oh what a tangled web we weave." The hard part of his work was being thrown into people's dirty laundry, and this would be very filthy indeed. John stepped outside to get a breath of fresh night air. He looked up and could see Sebastian watching him through a screen window. He wondered where the little owl might be. He had not dreamed of Kari for some time now. He would lie awake and think of her. Helen would have found her if it was at all possible. Nobody could have searched better, smarter, or longer. It would take a miracle. It was a dream.

John woke up Friday morning to his usual routine. "And a very good morning to you Sebastian. I guess I get to enjoy you for another day." John spent the morning pouring over his notes, and remembering the photo albums with such a happy family. Barbara had seen the pictures. She knew there were victims. How could Steven have let this happen? What did happen?

3PM came sooner than John wished, but he was ready.

"Right on time again, are you showing off?" Barbara turned on the charm, but it was so artificial. John shook her hand longer this time, playing it cool and friendly. Steven greeted him as well, with a good long handshake. Pictures flooded John's mind. He hoped he could retrieve them in more depth later.

Looking at houses John couldn't help but think of Kari. Could there ever be a chance he would be looking at houses with her? Barbara actually seemed to sense his thoughts. She spoke up. "Are you sure it's just you and that cat? Isn't there some special lady in your life?"

It couldn't hurt for John to play along, and he wouldn't lie. "I did meet somebody about a month ago. There was an attraction, but I haven't seen her since. She didn't give me her number."

Barbara spoke, but John saw her staring at Steven as the words came out. "When you see what you want you better do everything you can to make sure it doesn't get away. People can lead you on. I've always vowed nobody will do that to me. If somebody says they love me they better love me. That's all there is to it."

John felt uncomfortable the way she had been staring at Steven, but he knew Steven had to feel worse. All Steven could do was nod his head. He wouldn't disagree with Barbara, ever.

None of the townhouses interested John, but one of the single family homes really did catch his eye. He spoke of possibly having a family someday, though he was getting a bit old for that. He pressed Steven for details about family life.

"Family is a precious gift for those who deserve it," Steven spoke up. But Barbara would not let him ride far on his own train of thought. He had to share the seat with her.

Barbara spoke, "Steven really works hard for his family, but love is where you find it, not always where you expect it. Right Steve?" She challenged Steven with a strong glance.

"Whatever you say Barbara," Steven winked, but it was pathetic. John thought to himself, "You sure don't belong in any photo album now Mr. Richards." Thoughts of photography equipment had been flashing through his mind. Impressions were haunting John, drinks on a table, cameras, recording equipment. He wondered if Barbara might be recording their conversation. He would have some time sorting things out later, but he felt under surveillance. It was a creepy feeling he couldn't shake. The afternoon had gone as well as could be expected, and John got all the information to take with him about the one house he really did like. It was time to go for dinner.

After they arrived at the Black Bear bar and grill John and Steven got a table while Barbara went to freshen up. There was a good country ambiance in this place, and the food sure smelled very good. John grabbed the chance to grill Steven. "The past two nights we have been working through the dinner hour, how do you balance work and family life?"

Steven seemed a weak man. "I really don't do it very well. I used to. Well, I didn't used to work so hard. Having two kids to put through college is difficult."

John hit hard, "Steven, I have met your family. You are one of the luckiest men on earth I must say."

Steven was taken back. "Well thanks John, but things aren't always what they seem. Good fortune can turn on a dime. What seems like a dream come true one moment can turn into a living nightmare the next."

John took a shot at Steven, "Is Barbara your nightmare?"

Steven looked like he had seen a ghost.

"I think I heard my name. Are you two talking about me? I hope it's all good." Barbara was a piece of work. "I'm the lucky one tonight with two hunks at my table while so many girls have none." She was in her element and making the most of it.

"John gets the first dance." It was early, there was just a piano player playing softly, but another couple was dancing. "It's Okay John; Steven shares his help with our clients. Especially the handsome ones," she winked.

John played surrender, he would dance, and he would be careful. Barbara took his hand and led him over to the piano. She spoke to the piano player, "Hi Rick, this is John. He's helping Steve show me a good time tonight, not that Steve needs any help, you know what I mean. Any sign of Mark?"

"Haven't seen him in two days," Rick mentioned to Barbara.

"Well, tell him to call me if you see him." Barbara seemed somewhat concerned about who ever this Mark was.

John smiled at Rick. He never knew where his cases might take him, or what kind of people he would find. He really didn't want to be seen with Barbara, but nobody would know him. He thought about how it would be if Kari saw him now. The music was beautiful; he wanted Kari in his arms. Next thing he knew he realized Barbara was in his arms. "You can hold tighter than that?"

John put one hand behind Barbara's back, and held her other hand. The most difficult part of his cases can be making connections, he was getting a break here, but it wasn't pleasant. He toyed with Barbara. "You certainly have Steven's devotion," he let the words slip out.

"Steven knows what's good for him." She waved at Steven and winked. In Barbara's arms John was getting impressions, but they didn't make any sense. He sensed a news program, something about editing footage. He sensed something like Paparazzi. He saw crates of video tapes, and a news van. It was day dreaming, but more than that. He needed to remember all that he could for his notes.

Barbara called to Steven, "Getting jealous?" Steven shrugged. Barbara spoke again, condescending, "I better give him a turn. Thanks John." John felt cold. It was a physical chill that he got from Barbara. He was glad to be getting a break.

John tapped Steven's shoulder, "Better you than me."

Steven whispered back, "What did I do to deserve this?"

John fired back. "I'll show you someday."

John took a deep breath of relief when he got back to the table by himself. He smiled as he watched Steven and Barbara dance, but it was a forced smile. It felt very good to be by himself for a while. "What a night," he thought to himself. He was not feeling well now. There was something chilling about Barbara for sure. He couldn't be sure if it was that, or if he was suffering from something more serious. He watched Barbara take Steven's hand and place it on her thigh. Steven pulled back. It was all so uncomfortable. Barbara seemed to direct Steven's attention to John. John tried to just breathe and not think about what she could be saying. Barbara was a tricky sort. John was just drinking iced tea and Barbara seemed overly upset that he didn't order an alcoholic drink, even when he explained it as a medication issue. Most people would quickly let that drop, but at least five times through the evening Barbara kept suggesting at least one drink. John felt some impression of Barbara and drugs. He took mental notes as best as he could.

Barbara was certainly talking about John, but then she left to go somewhere and Steven returned to the table by himself.

"Hi," Steven said in kind of a pathetic tone. Dancing with Barbara was not something that left a man proud. After being with Barbara he tried not to draw attention to his embarrassment. John decided to stir the pot once more.

"You and Barbara don't look like such a happy couple." John looked Steven in the eyes intently.

Steven got defensive with more strength than he had shown up until now. "We are not a couple, I'm married."

John sighed and then spoke more softly, "Not happily married? Does Barbara know that?"

Steven spoke up with some force, "Barbara is interested in you John. We were talking, and she is impressed by you. She likes that you are determined in your dealings. If you would be interested in getting to know her better I can pretty well promise you she can get some rare deals in Real Estate. She has quite the connections."

John looked in Steven's eyes again, "I'm interested in her connection to you."

"Never mind that," Steven looked profoundly sad. "That's none of your business. Just remember what I said, get to know Barbara better and I'm sure she can lead to some sweet deals. You would not believe the sales she gets. I swear it is some kind of magic she uses. She gets her sights on some deal and the customers bite like fish on lures."

John would drop one last line, "I think you got one of Barbara's deals, and I'll pass."

Steven looked intently at John. He wondered just what John was after. It seemed like more than a house. John sensed his fear.

"Oh, still talking about me," Barbara bounced back to her seat. "Bet you're just patiently waiting your turn for another dance," Barbara squirted her words over John like she could mark him.

"Actually, I've got a cat to feed." John gave a friendly look of concern to Steven. The unspoken truth between them was that John could simply walk away, while Steven seemed to have no freedom at all.

Barbara fought it, "John, the night is young, I'm just getting to know you. I think I can really help you with your house searching. Don't you want another dance? We're just beginning to learn each other's moves, it gets more fun."

"I'm sorry, I do have a lot on my plate right now, and I better put something in my cat's dish soon." John looked at Steven and Barbara with appreciation. "Thank you both for all your efforts. I have some good listings to choose from. I can give this a lot of thought and call you when the time is right."

"Thank you for coming to us," Steven put out his hand. John held it more than shook it, looking in Steven's eyes, and trying to offer some hope.

"And thank you for dancing," Barbara gave him a kiss that did leave a mark. John promised to be in touch. As he left the bar and grill to catch a cab Barbara called out to him one last time, "See you soon." John waved back, looked at the two of them still out together when Steven at least should be home.

"In your dreams," John was free at last.

9

Dying

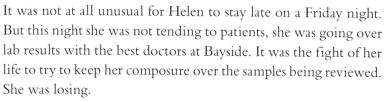

It was not at all unusual for Helen to stay late on a Friday night. But this night she was not tending to patients, she was going over lab results with the best doctors at Bayside. It was the fight of her life to try to keep her composure over the samples being reviewed. She was losing.

Dr. Bernard reviewed John's history with the other doctors and lab specialists present. Medical professionals often seem to go about their business free from emotional attachments, some out of necessity. Just the review of John's history took a half hour. Nobody in the room was emotion free after that. Tears streamed down Helen's face. She always tried to tell herself it wasn't that bad. She had just been thoroughly reminded that it was. When Dr. Bernard put his notes down there was quite a moment of silence.

Dr. Tom Brady was chief of staff among other things, and he had personally stayed to support Helen. "Helen the John Dreamer samples, from both visits, but especially this last visit, confirm leukemia. I'm very sorry. I know he's been a patient for a long time. But the bone marrow tests especially, this is just grim."

Helen put on the best show she could as a professional nurse of her stature.

"Yes, I've been caring for this patient for over five years.

51

I can't admire him more for the way he has faced cancer, and bounced back."

"You know there's no bouncing back from this." Dr. Brady didn't mince words.

Helen wiped back a tear as she stood concluding the gathering. "Thank you so much for reviewing this case with me. He's a special man and I just want to be sure he has the best care."

"He always has had the best care Helen. If I'm ever in his shoes I hope you'll be around." Dr. Brady was a truly good man.

While everyone left the building Helen stayed. Dr. Bernard lingered. He was very much the clinical expert, but not comfortable with interpersonal relationships. His respect and appreciation of Helen was immense. He had to say something.

"Helen I'm so sorry things look this bad. I'm glad so many people attended this meeting. You are the best nurse in the hospital. Nobody could have helped John more. None of it makes any sense. I have to say, and I'm sorry if this sounds very foolish, but I would have written John off five years ago. I don't know what has kept him going all this time. It has to have been your great care. I have felt bad over the years for betting against him. Just because it looks like a sure bet now, I'm not betting. Even if we have no hope, we don't have to take it away from John."

It may have been the best thing Dr. Bernard could have said, but Helen was not in a place to hear it. She kept hearing Dr. Brady's words, "You know there's no bouncing back from this." She thanked Dr. Bernard, but he could see his words had not sunk in. He just hoped they would in time.

Once she was finally alone she screamed. "This just can't be happening." For Helen it was a prayer, and she was going to give God what He deserved.

"John is the best man I've ever known, the kindest most loving human being I've ever heard of. You gave us a miracle, and now for what? And I actually start believing he might find Kari. Now what am I supposed to believe? I love that man. I can't be trying to keep him alive to find my daughter. But I can't let him go and leave me either. God I'm done!"

For years Helen had not been this shaken up in her life except for when John mentioned dreaming of Kari. But that actually woke a long dead hope. This had dealt all hope a death blow. Whatever their life had meant, whatever using this special discovery between them to repair broken dreams had been about, it was all coming to an end. Helen could not stop all the thoughts racing through her head. Maybe Kari was dead, and John was going to find her when he died.

"If that's the way it's gotta be." But it was all just too much to take in. Helen wished she had never become a nurse. She wished she had no idea what leukemia was, or what John would have to face now.

"I can't do it, you hear me?" It seemed as much her death sentence as John's, and Helen hated God at that moment more than she ever hated anything or anyone.

"If life is this unfair who wants it anyway? Go around killing people every day. What does this do for you?"

Deep down Helen knew she was in too much pain to be making any sense. All her words were just the voice of pain. What did she know? Dumb old woman just had the bad luck to love somebody, that's all. Helen had held the hands of the dying more than most. She would not leave the people who needed her. But this time she was feeling she needed John. She needed to be playing a part in the special mission they shared. Everything made them think it was a mission from God. Maybe it had just run its course. John and Kari belonged together. The only way to make any sense out of this was if death made that possible. But Helen couldn't let herself think that way. She kept reading over the test results, over and over. It was as if possibly they might change if she read them enough. She was never one to take sleeping pills before, but tonight she knocked herself out cold.

10

The Medicine

John felt like he had stepped into a new chapter of life when he got out of his car and looked at his humble home. It was like being sprung from prison. Sebastian was looking down through the window, making sure all was right with the world. "It is now," John thought to himself. But then he felt his life draining from him. The whole experience of a night out was very depressing. It had been a long time since John had been kissed by a woman, and John hated himself for kind of liking it. That is the power someone like Barbara can use. John could be vulnerable, but what about Steven? Steven had a precious wife. What power could Barbara have over him?

John sat on his front steps. He just sat there, not really able to even think. There were impressions to sift through and notes to write and sort, but right now he just let his mind go blank. It really wasn't a choice. He felt fried.

After a long silence, he heard Sebastian meow. "Oh my goodness, somebody has been very patiently waiting for dinner. I am so sorry buddy, we'll make it extra special." John gave Sebastian some cat treats and added some tuna to the usual meal. The big cat dug in and the motor started to roar. "That's my cat," John finally smiled.

John felt too beat to do anything but sleep. The work on

Susan's chart and the whole case would have to wait, but lying there would bring lots of thoughts to his already overloaded mind. He wanted to just flop on the bed, but he was the dreamer. He tucked everything tightly and squeezed himself in.

"Kari," John softly, reverently spoke out her name, and found himself instantly weeping. The thought of her was like light, revealing all the darkness to be nothing at all. That is what love does. It makes darkness nothing.

John found himself speaking. Speaking to Kari. He needed to be heard. "The only thing that matters should be something real, and not just a dream. Loving you is killing me. There is no point to any of this without you. How can we be apart?"

John's cries and prayers flowed out of him along with his consciousness until he slept as if dead. Not a sound, but he was still breathing.

It seemed as if he had slept the night, but it was only one hour into his sleep when he thought he was awakened. It was the bright green light. He couldn't focus on anything but green. He was wrapped in that glow. It was somehow comforting. In a short time it cleared. Then there was a sound, that precious sound that came from everywhere. John closed his eyes and didn't dare open them. Just keep listening, and maybe it will stay. He very slowly opened his eyes and found himself standing at the beginning of the boardwalk, just above the mist. He looked around in awe at that beautiful place, the most beautiful place he had ever seen. It was no less beautiful the second time, maybe even better. He saw where the boardwalk became a staircase leading up as far as the eye could see. Smaller falls threw their water like diamonds into the sunshine just to celebrate their beauty. He clutched the railing along the boardwalk and looked up as far as he could. He thought about the long climb ahead of him, and started to speak. "So I guess I better get started."

"Nope, I'm here."

John turned around and just melted. His heartbeat felt like a flash taking her picture. There was so much surrender just to look at her, but now he had something to say. "Kari."

Kari gazed in his eyes and beamed. They knew they both belonged in a picture. There should be a photo album with the two of them. But to John she was too beautiful for anything on earth to capture.

"Your Kari." She smiled at him and it made him glow. "You did good John, you are finding me."

John spoke, "Kari, it won't be soon enough, I'm dying without you. It gets worse every day. I did learn your name. I thank God every day for that. But how do I find you?"

Kari looked at him with the kind of love that is all that matters. It didn't matter if she would answer or not. It was breathtaking to look at her, and she seemed just as pleased to be looking at him. She rubbed her hand along the railing on her side of the boardwalk. Then she gazed in his eyes once more. It was impossible to tear his gaze from her eyes, but he noticed something. This time she had on a heart shaped silver necklace with an engraving. He stepped closer to see it. Everything once again became translucent. "No," Kari implored. John stepped back with his eyes shut praying with all his might to stay with her in this dream. He opened his eyes and she was still there. "Thank God," he whispered.

Kari spoke to him, "The necklace says "Nurses Are Patient People." I got it from work."

John looked at Kari with the most intense amazement he had ever felt. He pictured his wonderful nurse Helen, felt her rubbing her hand on his cheek to comfort him. Here was her daughter, a chip off the old block. He wept.

"What?" Kari spoke to him through a curious smile. "What is it John?"

John was almost as handsome as he could ever be. There was a weakness about him, but he was fighting it with intensity. He looked at Kari with all the love the world had ever known. "Kari, the reason falling in love hurts so much is because nothing you could ever do, and no gift you could give- could ever be enough to tell your beloved what you feel. But for you, when all I am feeling seems too much for any man to fathom, for you I have the most perfect beautiful gift there could be." He thought of Helen but wouldn't speak it.

"Then I guess you better find me," she said with that smile that made John feel as if he would melt away.

"There is a way to find me," she said. John was mesmerized as she stroked her hand over some ferns collecting all their moisture, then she placed her palm up in front of her and blew the spray over John blessing him. "Look at this place John. This is my kind of place. Do you know where we are?"

"Heaven." John confessed what he felt.

Kari burst out laughing, in that pure magical laugh that burst John's bubble every time. "Silly you. Heaven is not a place. It is the time we spend together. Look at this place John."

John giggled lightly in the magic of it all. "I'd rather look at you. Any other use of my eyes is wasted, but as you say." So John started to see where they were. Next to Kari was a square sign. Painted in blue was a bicycle with a line through it. There was to be no bicycle riding on the boardwalk. John was shocked. "This is a place." He looked all around. There were benches for people to sit who couldn't climb all the way at one time. There was a wooden trash receptacle. The stream at this point was surrounded by countless colorful leaves. There were humming birds darting in and out of flowers along the water's edge. This was a dream, but more than a dream. John walked a short way up the boardwalk taking in the incredible sights of this beautiful place. It was the only frame that could surround Kari, making her the perfect picture.

"This is amazing," John blurted out his astonishment.

"I know how to pick them." Kari boasted with every right.

John read a sign slightly back in the woods. There was to be no taking plants, wildflowers, insects, animals, rocks, or anything else out of the park.

John turned to Kari. "Someday I'd like to take you out of this park, to share my loved ones with my love. You are a miracle Kari. I don't know how this can be, but even if it is just a dream I will live it all my days searching for you until my final breath."

Kari stood before him in the full glory of the beauty God had given her, and with as much love as God's to give John back.

Everything that happened with Kari was a miracle. Just her existence was more a gift than any man could deserve to see. Any common place action if it involved her would always be living in a dream. The wonder of it all was not wasted on John. The man who thanked God for every breath was thanking God with his whole being for being able to look at this beautiful Kari. But there was more to miracles than even he knew.

Kari spoke, "I have something for you John. You said you were dying without me, but love doesn't take life, it gives life. You are very sick. You need me more than you know. I am a nurse."

John was astounded, excited, fearful, and it all blended with hopelessly in love. He didn't dare speak of Helen yet. He didn't know what this dreaming experience with Kari was all about or where it could lead. Where was it leading now?

"I have a great nurse." John dared to say it.

Kari looked at him with a familiar but more intense love than he had ever seen in beautiful eyes. "You need what only I can give you, just as I need you." She held out her hand and opened it up to John. There was a pill that looked like a glowing diamond. "Take this John." She pointed to the waterfall. "You must take it with plenty of water. Go in to the water, wade over to the falls, and take this pill. I made it myself."

Kari set the pill on the railing. John picked it up. He could not feel physical sensations, but he saw the pill was in his hand. He sat down on the edge of the board walk and slipped in to the water. He waded over to the falls as Kari had said. He put the pill in his mouth and cupped his hands in the falls, filled them with the water, and drank it swallowing the pill. He waded back over and climbed back up onto the boardwalk.

"Good boy," Kari seemed so pleased. They beamed at each other as only lovers can.

"What was that?" John asked.

"Fusheeswa," Kari answered looking as if she had revealed an ancient sacred secret.

John stood there overcome with the wonder and amazement of it all. He wanted to say something, but could find no words.

"Find me John." Kari's face once again took on that sad look he couldn't bear to see. Once again a tear, then another, slipped from her perfect eyes.

She was losing her composure. She had been so happy that he took his medicine, but now she was failing.

"I need you John."

"Have some faith." John gave his love, letting her know he would do whatever it takes to find her.

She lifted her hands as if in prayer, and then to catch something- the owl.

John grabbed the covers over himself just in time as Sebastian landed on him on his way to the window. Then with two paws the big cat batted at the window like a drummer. The owl was off on its way.

11

Prepare To Dream

John was soaked. He didn't know if the water from wading over to the falls had carried over from his dreaming to his waking state, or if a fever had broken.

"Fusheeswa. A miracle drug. It would be a miracle if I spelled it right." John struggled out of his tightly wrapped sheets, got up and wrote that name down with his best guess at the spelling. With that name written down he could go back to bed and get a little more sleep before facing whatever lay before him. He rinsed his face and dried himself with a towel before lying back down. He lay there thanking God for the precious gift of the best dreams any man could experience. Finding Kari would top all. He believed in this dream. So much wonder had happened so fast, yet it seemed as if he had been searching for Kari for ages. He had been starting to lose faith, but a fresh dream brought new hope. He had no idea how badly Helen needed hope. He would find out.

He lay there for a while, enjoying the rest, but with dreams like his running through his mind there would be no more sleeping. The good mixed with the bad as he remembered Kari's pain. She was deeply pained, perhaps by being alone. Dreaming of her had brought loneliness to John's reality, perhaps she felt that too.

"I guess I get to enjoy you for another day," John stroked Sebastian's head and listened to the purring. "You are too spoiled," John let the big cat know the score.

John had breakfast and got ready for his day. He took his vitamins. He had planned on going over the Richard's case all day, but another dream of Kari made it impossible for him to focus on anything but her for a while. Either way he would need Helen. He called the hospital but found she was not at work.

"I hope everything's alright." John spoke out to himself. Sebastian nudged him as if to offer some support. John noticed he felt lighter, like some weight he was carrying had been lifted. He didn't know what it was, but he really felt good today. Any dream of Kari would do that, but she had given him medicine. What was that about? He wrote that name Fusheeswa down on another piece of paper and put it in his wallet. Feeling this good, and this keyed up, only a walk would do.

It was a very good day for walking. Warmer weather was on the way. "Springtime is for lovers," he whispered to himself. He never thought he would be one, but he was a dreamer. This latest dream would haunt him a long time. Where was that place? Was it a real place on Earth? He thought he would take a little time in the library searching on the computer for parks, boardwalks, waterfalls. Before he knew it hours had past and he was nowhere. He would not find Kari by earthly means. If it only cost him one day of life to learn that lesson it was worth it.

When he got back home after a long walk he did pour over his notes, pondering what had become of Steven Richards. Steven was a man who had his love, a love one finds in dreams. But Steven was throwing it away. What was he afraid of? His children deserved their father's attention. How could Steven waste his time with Barbara? John would find out, and Steven would find out too.

The next day Helen was still not available. John wasn't ready just yet, but he couldn't repair a dream without Helen. He didn't want to. The special relationship they had, the wondrous secret they shared, made their experiences something beautiful and sacred for both of them. Helen had not called John in need of help. Maybe she just wasn't feeling well. A woman can take some days off.

Days went by with no word from Helen and no response to phone calls. It would take a long time for John to get accustomed to his new-found health. "Maybe forever," he even murmured to himself. But he grew more concerned for Helen with every passing day.

John called Susan and arranged to meet with her again. With Steven always working late it was easy to go visit her any time. Susan was such a beautiful person. The intense emotions of broken dreams and his sensitive nature gave John strong feelings for the people he wanted to help. He had to be sensitive, to feel what people feel, know what people know, get inside their most personal dreams. It was sacred ground. John prayed to be kept in the hands of grace, to have faith, to live faith, to use whatever gift was his to give for a greater good. He would take whatever effort necessary to stay as pure in heart as possible. Even on a Friday night Steven was away. Steven and Barbara had more meetings with customers. John remembered his meetings, and Barbara. This would be a much better evening for him, but it certainly should be Steven spending time with Susan and their family on a Friday night.

Saturday was Danny's birthday. Steven had promised to be there for his party, so perhaps it was more understandable that he had to clear things up Friday night.

When John rang the bell Danny and Caitlin seemed as eager to see him as Susan. John felt mobbed as a daddy should be. "Well I'm very happy to see you both again," John beamed in the light of childhood joy.

"Will you read us a story?" The kids were too precious.

"What would you like?" John smiled at Susan. There were

no words between them, but they both knew the children should hear a story.

"The Little Engine That Could."

John read the story with much feeling. He would have made a good father. He wondered about family with Kari. Kari could make him lose focus too easily. The Richard's family needed him now. Any personal thoughts would have to go.

"Alright now, thank Mr. Dreamer and get to bed." Susan was a wonderful mother. It helps to have wonderful children.

Caitlin broke the pleasant mood with the innocent question of a loving child. John could hardly breathe when she spoke the words, "Can you be my new daddy? I want a daddy that reads to me."

There was a long uncomfortable silence before John could find any words to respond. "Caitlin, you have the luckiest daddy in the world. He is lucky because he has the best daughter there could be. He used to read to you all the time. Your Mommy has pictures of him reading to you and Danny. I think he just needs to be reminded to read to you."

"Okay now guys, time for bed. Thank Mr. Dreamer like I said." Susan fought back tears but kept to the business of parenting.

"They can call me John," John was very comfortable with Susan and the kids.

John knew he had to get down to business and prepare Susan for what lay ahead. "Susan, you have a beautiful dream. You and the kids deserve the best. I have to admit I'm disappointed in Steven, even a bit jealous." John would hold to sacred ground, but that was a compliment he wanted to give. He wanted Susan to know it wasn't her that was breaking dreams. "The worst thing people do is give in to fear. It is what makes people their own worst enemies. If only people knew that living in fear is worse than what they are afraid of, so much suffering could be avoided. Fear is the sin. I've gotten to know Steven. Repairing a dream is serious business. I need to be thorough. This will be no band aid.

It will be more like surgery, and with instructions for life style changes. I believe Steven and I will discover what he is afraid of, but Steven will need to learn to stop being afraid."

Susan was totally focused on everything John said. "I've loved Steven so much from the moment I laid eyes on him. I'd give my life for him. What can I do to help this?" Susan started to cry.

John handed her the tissues. "It's Okay. Actually, there is something. Susan, do you remember your dreams each night?"

"Not usually. Sometimes I have a nightmare, like after the bus accident. Sometimes I know I've had a dream but can't remember what it was about."

"You are not alone Susan," John spoke with her like a doctor would. "Most people do not dream as well as they should. In today's world with all the fast foods and everything so filled with sugar, people do not get enough B vitamins. Susan, I can't go into much detail about what I do or how I do it, but I work in people's dreams. If people can't dream properly I can't help them. I seriously need you to give your family, but especially Steven, very good nutrition and B vitamin supplements. Steven will especially need B6 vitamins. You can tell the family you are on a health kick, do the research. However you do it is up to you, but I have to know Steven is getting a good dose of B6. If he will just take it that's fine. If you need to mix it in food, do it. Call me in a week and let me know if this is working. You will all start remembering your dreams. It may seem very strange at first, but it is the right thing to do."

"I want to do it." Susan was very sincere. "I've honestly thought about how we should be taking vitamins. I've talked about it. This should work. I'll just explain I'm sorry I've been putting it off and I want to get everyone healthy."

"Great," John was pleased, and relieved to get a good idea that this would work.

"There's something else Susan. I know it may seem crazy, but this is my business. I want you to tuck the sheets in very tightly.

Not too ridiculous, but do the best job you can of making the bed you sleep in. I want Steven to have to squeeze in to it. I want the covers tight. When his body is more confined during his sleep his mind will seek escape. He will dream deeper. That is what we need. Are you okay with this?"

"John this makes sense, what you're saying. You're the expert. I just don't know how anything can make this better." She started to tear up again. She was so beautiful even in sorrow. It was so moving to be there with her. John wanted to take her in his arms and hold her close for comfort. It took such effort to keep his feelings clear.

"Susan, at some point Steven will have a dream that shows him what he has done with your dream. Something very terrible has happened to Steven. He is a lost man who has forgotten about dreaming. To get him to dream he will need a wakeup call. It sounds ironic, but I think I'm right about this. If your dream is yours and Steven's, and if he can learn to put it ahead of fear, you will share a most precious gift you must guard always."

"That is what we had John. Or what I thought we had. I just want it back." Susan was so sweet. It took a lot of emotional energy to do his work, but John felt motivated by Susan and her beautiful children. It was worth a shot.

John shook Susan's hand as he left her house. Before either of them knew it she was in his arms. There was a timeless moment, and everything seemed so silent.

In a flash John was in the nail salon. He watched as Susan's friend Peggy spoke up with such brightness in her voice, "Susan Richards I can't believe it. God how long has it been? Why do we let so much time slip away?"

Susan's reply with such feeling, "Gosh I don't know I just know it is so good to see you. Thank God you were here today of all days."

"Well its Saturday honey- that will do it. Come here on a Saturday and you've found me."

Susan's tears hurt John, he snapped back to the present.

It felt like they both discovered what had happened at the same time, and used equal effort to pretend it was not a big deal. John wiped a tear from his eye and Susan did the same. John felt a need to lighten this moment fast. If he slipped back in her arms he would never leave.

"He pointed at her like a concerned serious teacher, "B6."

"I'll pick it up tomorrow, I promise, lots of it." Susan stayed at the door and waved at John as he drove away. He waved back. He felt grateful to have some connection with this special person. He was a privileged man. It was unsettling that he couldn't remember how she ended up in his arms. They both needed a hug. That must be it.

It was late, but driving home John got to thinking just how good he felt. Kari must be some amazing nurse. She and Helen were both wizards with medicine. John put his window down and breathed the fresh air. Then the weirdest thing happened to him, he got a coffee craving. He thought to himself, "This never happens, but why not be like a normal human being and stop and get a cup of coffee?" There was a convenience store up ahead and John was determined to go for it.

Walking in John was surprised at how many people were in the store so late. He found where the coffee was dispensed. A tall distinguished gentleman was ahead of him pouring himself a coffee. When he went to get a lid he dropped his newspaper. John bent over to pick it up as a nice gesture. When he looked the man in the face he recognized the face but couldn't quite pick up the name. The man obviously recognized John and spoke.

"John Dreamer?"

John answered, "Yes," and looked at him intently trying to get the name.

"I'm Dr. Brady from Bayside Medical Center."

"Oh yes." John held out his hand. It was an innocent gesture, but when Dr. Brady grasped his hand John felt impressions shoot through his body. It was fear about Helen. It was against John's nature to be impulsive, and he felt humbled in the presence of a great doctor, but John blurted out his question. "Is Helen alright?"

Dr. Brady came across as a father figure, perhaps larger than life. He looked at John with great concern, with compassion for people, but also a professional assurance. He spoke with a deep clear voice. "Helen is very fond of you John. She's taking this very hard. I've never seen her like this over a patient before. You've made quite an impression on her. She has taken some time off. I hope she returns soon."

John couldn't help but look shocked. He reviewed the words in his head, "She's taking this very hard." He thought to himself, "Taking what very hard?" Dr. Brady obviously thought John knew whatever it was he was talking about. It must be something Helen was supposed to have told him. Why didn't she tell him? What could it be?

Dr. Brady interrupted John's thoughts, "How are you feeling John?"

John was putting two and two together. Kari had said he was sick, and she had taken care of him. John felt a smile coming on, all the more meaningful because he would be speaking the truth. "Dr. Brady, I can honestly say I have never felt better." John let the words break over Dr. Brady's perplexed face. "I am sure looking forward to a cup of Joe."

Dr. Brady put on a brave front, "I'm very glad you're feeling well. Go easy on that coffee."

When John got out to his car it was a special moment, getting that first sip of a good cup of coffee. He relished the moment, but quickly got back to the impressions from Dr. Brady. He was very worried about Helen. The two of them knew something of how sick John had been, and he didn't even know what that was about. For Helen to be unable to talk about it with him must mean it was very bad. John remembered the look on Kari's face when he had taken her pill, the look of a nurse who was saving a life, and glad for the opportunity. John knew the precious gift of repairing broken dreams. Helen must be suffering a broken dream herself. He felt terrible that she would be suffering. He hoped he could find her tomorrow morning and clear things up. It was very late now and hopefully Helen would be sleeping. John said a prayer to Kari, "Help me find our angel tomorrow and tell her I'm Okay.

12

Have Some Faith

John woke up the next morning, Saturday, to the sound of Sebastian pawing at the window. He had not dreamed of Kari but wondered if the owl had been there.

"Good morning Sebastian. I guess I get to enjoy you for another day, maybe a lot of days."

John sat up in bed and realized just how good he felt. "This is amazing," he thought to himself. He vowed he would not take anything for granted. He would never stray from a healthy life style. He would take his vitamins, keep his hospital appointments, and get more blood work for sure. A cup of coffee once in a while couldn't hurt. He was still surprised at last night's craving. He gazed out the window every which way, but there was no sign of an owl. Thinking of blood tests got him back to thoughts of Helen. He did have her phone number. The phone went unanswered and John left a message for her to please call. He mentioned that he was feeling fine and had things to tell her.

Helen could hardly move. She couldn't pick up the phone. Tears just poured from her eyes as she heard John's voice. "The calm before the storm," Helen wept the words. She just could not bear the thought of what John would be going through. It was too unfair to contemplate. She had become such a mixture of sadness and anger she was paralyzed.

"What is up with Helen?" John spoke the words, and looked at Sebastian intently as if waiting for him to explain it.

John tried the hospital hoping Helen was back at work. She sometimes worked Saturdays, but he learned she was still out on her leave of absence. This was serious. He called her home again. "Helen its John, I've really got to talk to you, I'm Okay."

Helen shook her head. She wanted to crawl under a rock and die. "What you don't know- will hurt you," she spoke at the phone message recorder. She lay down on her bed and hugged the pillow tightly. She felt like a little child wishing her mother could come and make everything better. "Have some faith," she heard her mother say. "I see where faith gets us now," Helen's bitterness flowed out of her. She had had enough of being the nice sweet lady giving all the love she had to give only to lose a daughter, and now the closest thing to a son she would ever know.

After giving his cat plenty of food and water John paced back and forth for a while. He looked over his notes on the Richards family. He looked at a picture of Steven Richards on a Richard's Realty flyer. He spoke to it as if he was speaking to Steven, "What you don't know, will hurt you, but it might also help."

One more time, he called Helen's number. "Helen, don't make me come over there, please call me."

Helen shook her head, "Oh God leave me alone." The last thing she wanted was to see John all happy and have to give him a death sentence in return for his love. John seemed happy on the phone. Maybe he had had another dream of Kari. Maybe death would get them together. Maybe John would not have to wait as long as Helen had, but Helen would lose everybody. There was nothing for her to look forward to, and everything to escape from.

"Have some faith," John spoke the words as if to himself and Sebastian as he started for the door. His normally silent cat let out quite a meow. It was as if he had given an answer. John was startled, but replied. "Okay then."

As John was driving toward Helen's house he passed the

billboard for the health club. "A Perfect Body Is Waiting For You." John shook his head thinking of Kari's breath taking beauty. There was something different about looking at Kari. He loved Kari. It was more than something he felt, more than something he hoped for. Loving Kari somehow defined him. He could only shake his head at everything that was happening. He felt like he suddenly had the perfect body himself. Kari was so sacred to him, but his new found physical health affected him in new ways. He found himself wanting Kari, wanting to feel her in his arms, wanting to hold her close and feel her physical body against his. "Don't dream and drive," he remembered his close call. The two best nurses were looking after him. He better be careful. He needed to help the older one.

John drove up in front of Helen's house and parked the car. He said a prayer before unfastening his seat belt. There was some mail in the mail box. It looked like Helen had not even picked up her mail for the last few days. John rang the door bell and waited. There was no sign of life. He opened the storm door and knocked on the front door a few times. He rang the bell again. Finally, he walked around the house, calling out at each window. "Helen Weiss? Mail delivery for Helen Weiss. We have mail for Nurse Weiss." "Well?," he went back to the front door and knocked and knocked. "Helen I'm not leaving. I need to talk to you. Why won't you answer the door? It's John Dreamer. It's your friend."

The door very slowly opened. Helen was fully dressed and had her coat on. John had never seen her look this bad, and he had seen her with the flu once. "Helen I've been very worried about you. What's going on?"

Helen put up her hand. "John I just can't talk about it. I can't even think straight. I'm not ready for this," she started crying. "I can't do this now."

She couldn't help noticing something different about John. He looked like the picture of health, and he was calm and assured. It was everything she was afraid of; he was doing very well as patients can before the full fury of leukemia hits. She didn't want to ruin what precious time he had left. She cried out louder this time, "I can't," and passed John on her way out her door and out to the street.

John shook his head and looked intently at her as she walked away. "What is going on?" he muttered to himself. "Well, at least I'm up for this now."

Helen looked back briefly and saw John coming after her. She quickened her pace. Thoughts streamed through her mind, including terrible guilt for causing John to strain himself coming after her. She wished he would give up. What could he be thinking?

John wasn't about to tackle her. He would just keep up with her for as long as it would take.

Helen abruptly stopped. She stared at him with less than love. "Will you stop?" She asked with quite an angry expression.

John gazed at her with penetrating love. "Helen, we need to talk."

With all her strength Helen just yelled in his face, "I can't."

She took off again toward Bayside. She was approaching busier parts of the city. John watched her for a while as she gained distance. He started after her again, keeping his distance this time.

Helen scurried down a busy street which opened into a large piece of property. She darted into a church building. John approached intently and deliberately. He didn't feel strained at all, but he did wish for this strange chase to end. A church might be a good place. He walked up the steps and started inside, reading the brass sign- St. Mary's Roman Catholic Church. John crossed himself on the way in, not even knowing it was the right thing to do until he did. That was frequently how life worked. Do the right thing and you will know it. He felt in the right, and he felt such love for Helen. She needed to stop running from whatever it was that had her in such a state.

It was a very beautiful church, and Helen obviously knew it

well. She knew where she was going. John wasn't Catholic, but he figured the room Helen entered was a confessional. She slammed the door. He figured out how he could go in where the priest would sit to hear the people confess their sins. He would be very close to her in there. She might just bolt, or maybe she had had enough. He took his place.

"You don't belong here." Helen used a hushed but serious voice.

"I belong with you." John's voice was almost mystical. Words of love that pure hit their mark. There was a very long silence before John spoke again. "Helen, I know you're worried about me. I'm Okay. I'm more worried about you. Dr. Brady is worried about you.

"You're not Okay." Helen's voice cried out those painful words. Words she had not been able to say. She couldn't bear this. "Oh God," she cried out. "I'm so sorry. I'm so sorry."

John could hear her weeping from the confessional. "Helen I need to talk to you. I'm really alright. I had another dream. I saw Kari. Helen, she knew I was sick. She gave me medicine."

"Leukemia." Helen screamed that word from hell and it knocked John down on the bench in his side of the confessional. It seemed to echo.

"It's Leukemia John. What miracle drug did Kari give you for that?" Helen collapsed in a flood of tears. She had hit him with it, full force. She felt as if she herself had killed him.

John sat there in shock. Minutes passed with no sound. The reality of it all slowly sank in to his mind, but there was much he still didn't know. "What did Kari give me for that?" He pondered a miracle. He reached into his wallet and pulled out the crinkled piece of paper, unfolded it, and looked at the word. He would give it his best shot, and try to pronounce it exactly as Kari had. He stood up again and strained to see Helen as he said it to her. "Fusheeswa."

Fusheeswa. The word was like rain falling down on a parched

barren desert, bringing it to life when it had appeared too late. She only had to hear that word, and she could once again see that she was in the arms of love. The greatest love. And she always had been. It just couldn't be, but she believed the unbelievable. She had heard John say it. John said it. Kari gave him her Fusheeswa. All her love wrapped up in a special medicine just for him. She had to be her daughter. John had to be Okay. She, Helen, should have some faith.

John felt good about the long silence. Helen had not said a thing. She did not ask about the word, she did not question his sanity. Maybe he shouldn't either. John left his side of the confessional and waited to see if Helen would come out. The door ever so slowly did open. She was all cried out, but Helen was the second most beautiful thing he had ever seen. There was a weak smile through the tears. God's rainbow John thought to himself.

This time Helen spoke the word, and he was relieved he had pronounced it correctly. "Fusheeswa. So you got Kari's Fusheeswa."

Wow, Helen had been changed in an instant by that word. John weekly asked, "Leukemia?"

"Forget about it." Helen seemed obviously Okay. She was getting her life back. And how do you deal with a miracle?

"Good stuff?" John looked in her eyes with inquisitive eyes himself.

"The best," Helen beamed. "All you ever need."

Without a thought John blurted out, "Is it legal?"

Life and death had hung in the balance for too long. The pressures had been something nobody should ever have to face. With that crazy question the dam burst. Helen exploded with laughter. It was the greatest music John could have heard in the church that day. It was contagious, and the two of them were on the floor before they knew it. When they did realize it, it was just that much more funny. It seemed like God's greatest mercy when they could finally lie quietly and breathe normally. Cried out, and now laughed out, it was one hell of a day.

John helped Helen to her feet, and she looked at a stained glass window. "Love bears all things, believes all things, hopes all things, endures everything." 1 Corinthians 13: 7. She held John in her arms like the son that he was. John said it first, "I love you Helen." There couldn't have been many tears left, but there were a few as Helen said it back.

"I just need a minute before we leave. A minute for a prayer," Helen said.

"Take two," John said back with new found spirit.

When they finally left the church John had to ask, "Can we please just walk back?"

13

The Long Walk Home

When John and Helen walked out the front entrance to the church Helen looked out over the parking lot. "Now where did I park my car?" She was joking, but John played along.

"Conveniently in your garage."

"Oh that's right, you asked if we could please just walk back. Okay then."

The two of them giggled for a moment, and it felt precious to be normal. Though normal is quite a relative term, and neither one of them thought of John and his gifts as normal. The trip to the church had been an emotional blur. The trip home was a long walk. There were still rays of sun though it was getting much lower in the sky. It was a good thing Helen wore her coat. In spite of the sun there was a chill in the air. No matter what the calendar may say. Spring had been pushed back for a time. It would be possible to walk at a good clip without causing a sweat.

John pointed out to Helen, "You lead the way, this is your turf."

"Fine," Helen smiled, "I lead, and you choose the topic of conversation."

There was silence for a few minutes. Helen glanced at John with an inquisitive look.

"I'm thinking."

Helen spoke up, "Alright I'll talk. I guess I have a lot bottled up. I've been a basket case. I don't know what happened."

She stopped and looked in John's eyes intently. "But John, your blood work was conclusive. The best doctors at Bayside reviewed everything with me. God they gave such support, staying late on a Friday, letting their families wait."

It was very serious, and it had become quite public. "The best doctors at Bayside think you're a dead man. I thought so." Helen started tearing up again. "For five years I've fought to keep you alive. I know it has been worse for you, but I was doing my best caring for you. We're not supposed to have favorites Hell. We're not supposed to get emotionally attached- Hell. Now this time it is Leukemia staring at me in the charts, on the computer screens, and in the eyes of my colleagues. I've been all caught up in taking care of you and how much you need me. Losing you I felt my world collapse. I didn't know how much I needed you. The dream repair business is just a miracle any way you look at it. When we are working together I feel so close to God there are no words. But I thought God was taking you away, and even if it was to take you to Kari I hated Him. I hated Him bad."

John gave Helen another big hug. Helen and John were family now. There was growing comfort between them, and no turning back. It was John's turn to speak.

"We all have such lessons to learn of faith every day. God knows I am trying to convince myself every morning that I actually have some chance of finding Kari. Oh Helen, the dreams...the dreams. She is so beautiful and precious. I can't even begin. And she is sad. It breaks my heart. If the doctors listen to my heart they might hear it crying. So maybe there is some way I could help her. Some reason I should find her in my dreams, and some purpose in looking for her. I think it's to bring her to you."

There was a picnic table in a small park just off the road. Helen walked over and sat down. They had been walking quite a while, and her emotions made her weak.

"John I'll just keep praying. I've been praying for Kari for a lifetime. I'm afraid to hope. I'm afraid to have faith, because it is so good- and I don't want to lose it. I'm so sorry I lost it, but darn it- I'm a nurse. I've studied medicine- hard and long. I know how the body works. Chemotherapy, vitamins, hormones, mineral levels, antibiotics, these are my life. This has been the way of life for me, and it is what I do to help people. I can't believe everything I feel now. I feel jealous. I work this hard, and Kari just gives you a pill and you're fine. Or are you?"

John sat down across from Helen. Helen couldn't help but notice how handsome he looked. The setting sun was definitely his light. John looked at his right hand, made a fist, and opened it again. He held it up like he was receiving life, soaking it up in that hand as he looked at the setting sun. Helen believed that was exactly what he was doing. He smiled at Helen again.

"Helen," He looked down at the ground for a bit, then back in her eyes. "Life is everything. All of it. Too much for us mere earth folks to peg, but I feel it. I feel it now more than ever. All of it Helen. I would not be alive if it wasn't for countless things you did to keep me here. If any piece was missing in this puzzle I'd have been gone years ago. You know what you do, and it is a secret between you and God. Those potions of yours. You got me dreaming Helen. That is the only way I could have found Kari. And you," he paused to catch enough breath to speak it; "You brought Kari into this world. She got Fusheeswa from you."

Helen smiled. She was feeling better. They were most of the way to her home. Being with John in this real setting, not an emergency in a hospital, was more therapeutic than she could have imagined. They would have to figure out what the relationship would be from here. Did he need to be a patient? Was he completely cured? Did dream repairs still require her potions? Could he do them now? It was a lot of questions, but she only asked him one.

"Any ideas how you're going to find Kari?"

In some ways it was the only question either of them ever had. It was what made life a question. What could he say?

"Well, she wants me to find her. She needs me for something. I think I need her more than I'll ever understand. It is amazing feeling this good, this healthy. Do normal people feel this way all the time? I hope it lasts. I want Kari in my life. I feel like I always have. Helen, she showed me something of where she is. I think it is a place on earth where she goes sometimes. A healing place. A place that is the only frame beautiful enough to hold her. There were signs there, written in English." John looked at Helen with a shy expression, almost asking her permission to hope. Then he spoke the profound half joke that had been haunting him. "I think I'll be safe in limiting my search to the North American Continent."

Helen nodded in weak agreement. It takes a lot of strength to hope.

14

Magic

When Helen and John reached the house it was now pretty dark. They stopped and looked at each other, love and grins.

"I'll call you Monday Helen," John spoke with a smile. "I guess I need a follow up visit. There does seem to be a change in my condition. I also think we need to follow the same dream protocol. It is getting close to time for me to attempt a repair."

John had no idea how close it was for a necessary dream. He would find out very soon.

"Welcome back from the dead John. You better not ever get any ideas of leaving me. You are my son, and if God be with us we'll make that "son in law." If you got Kari's Fusheeswa and it really did the trick it is going to turn Bayside upside down. I had everybody and their brother review your blood work. I don't know what we can tell them, but not about Fusheeswa. But you know what we need to do?"

John glowed for a moment, and revealed he did know. "Have some faith."

John took a long scenic route home. He drove by a lake with beautiful lamps all around it. He could see there were ducks by a fountain near a gazebo. For a moment he thought about being in that gazebo with Kari. He made up his mind an evening walk with her around that lake would be one of the first things to do if he could ever bring her home. "Bring her home," he heard himself say. He looked at the near full moon rising above the hills along his way. Kari could be looking at that moon. She had to be somewhere. It was such an emotional day. He had lost his parents in an accident so long ago, but now he did have a mother indeed. An angel who just needed a reminder that truth is stranger than fiction.

He had not given much mind to the time, but he did notice his car dash board clock said it was 10:45PM as he approached his home street. "Sebastian must be ready for a snack," he thought to himself. As he approached his home he was shocked to see a white BMW SUV in front of his apartment. He saw the license plate, REAL T. His senses jumped into overdrive. This was Susan's car. What could she possibly be doing here?

He pulled up and parked behind her. She was in the driver's seat waiting, hoping he would come home. John got out of his car and slowly walked toward her. He was focused on her completely. He did not notice far down the road a TV news van parked in the shadows.

"Susan," he spoke softly through her open window.

"John," Susan was weeping. "I'm sorry. I don't know what to do. I needed to get away. I don't know who to turn to, and you're the only one I can trust with this. I need you John. I'm sorry."

John opened her car door and led her by the hand out of the car. She wept and he held her tight, praying to give her what comfort she may need.

Barbara had asked the piano player at the club if he had seen Mark. The mention of his name had passed without incident. John never gave it a thought. In the TV news van down the street a high-powered light sensitive camera was focused on the scene. "Susan in the arms of John, how sweet it is," murmured Mark Cason. "This should be a productive night."

"Susan what's wrong?" John looked at her with such love

and concern. Susan held her hands over her mouth as if it was too painful to talk.

"Let's go inside." John held out his hand and Susan took it. "You need to sit down and relax. I'll fix you some tea." He looked at her with such feeling coming from his caring eyes. "And you get to meet Sebastian."

They walked up the stairs and into John's apartment. His curtains were open, letting in fresh spring air. The news van pulled up closer. It would be no trouble to capture what went on inside.

John put the kettle on the stove. He and Susan sat at his dining table. He put out both hands and she took them.

"Oh John, today was Danny's 7th birthday. We planned for weeks. I wanted it to be so special. I wanted Steven there, and he promised he would be." Susan was a crying mess. John gave her tissues. He shook his head.

"I'm so sorry Susan. You are a wonderful mother, and a wonderful wife. Why wasn't Steven there?"

"It was another last minute meeting. He said this involved a million dollar home sale. John, he asked me if Danny's birthday was worth a million dollars. I don't know what to say. I don't want to be a stupid wife. What is wrong with me?"

John shut his eyes. This beautiful woman just wanted a normal life and a happy birthday party for her son. Why did a million dollar home sale depend on events that day? John served the tea, and he put his loving arms around Susan.

"Nice, let's have a kiss." Mark's heart, if he could be said to have one, was pounding with excitement. This filming assignment was going very well. "Too bad I don't have sound, but it's pretty obvious what we have here. Barbara was right as usual. She is going to love me." He adjusted the focus, shot after shot of John and Susan together.

John held Susan's hands. He shut his eyes. He could see in his mind's eye the birthday party. He could hear Danny crying,

"Where's Daddy? He promised Mommy, he promised he would be here." John saw Susan do her best to hide her tears at that party. He saw how tired she was of making excuses. It didn't get easier with practice, it got worse. It was getting too hard to put on the show at all. With his eyes still shut, John saw Susan standing at the waterfall where Kari stood. It shocked him and he opened his eyes and looked into hers. All he could see was the sadness.

They sat there hand in hand not knowing what to say. John shook his head. Susan needed to wipe more tears away.

Out in the news van Mark watched everything unfold through his camera lens.

"Oh go ahead and kiss her. You know you want to. Let's get this show on the road." Mark had no idea about the nature of love. He would never get the picture.

Suddenly Sebastian jumped at the window. John instantly thought of the owl and rushed to look out. But when he got to the window he slipped into a trance. It all happened in just an instant. John stood there in a dream. He was in the club with Steven listening to him talk about Barbara. John relived every moment, every detail. He heard every word Steven said.

"You would not believe the sales she gets. I swear it is some kind of magic she uses. She gets her sights on some deal and the customers bite like fish on lures."

John was suddenly back to reality. No owl, but he saw the news van right in front of his house.

"Shit," Mark knew he had been spotted. He secured the camera, but had to get out of the back of the van and around to the driver's seat.

"Wait here," John yelled at Susan before rushing out his door. John had all the health of an athlete now. He heard the back door of the van slam shut as he ran down his steps and across the street. Then the driver's side door slammed. It started up, and Mark got ready to pull out as John reached the driver's side door. "Stop," John yelled. He grabbed at the door handle, but the van was taking off. John couldn't touch Mark, but he had grabbed the door handle right after Mark had shut the door.

"You lose," Mark laughed as he floored it. John couldn't stop a van, but he did hang on for a moment, and he punched near the driver's side rear quarter panel as the van slipped away, and thought he may have left a dent. "Bayside News 7," it said on the side of the van, and John got part of the plate number, 417.

John stood there in the street watching the van fade from view. It felt like standing in a dream. Susan ran up to him. "What is it John? What happened?"

John was bent over holding his knees. He had expended a lot of energy to get to that driver's side door so fast.

John held his left hand that had pounded on the side of the van and stared at the van as it vanished from sight. Then he looked deep in Susan's eyes. "I just discovered magic."

15

Marty

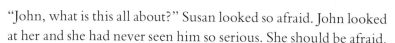

"John, what is this all about?" Susan looked so afraid. John looked at her and she had never seen him so serious. She should be afraid.

"Susan we need to go back inside and talk." Susan wiped a tear away from her right eye and took his arm. As he led her up the stairs she noticed his energy for the first time. Once inside she took a better look at him. He had always been somewhat handsome, but she remembered now that he had been rather frail. She got a shocked expression on her face as she realized just how much John had changed.

"John, you look so different."

"Is that good or bad?"

"I just remember you being, I don't know, kind of frail. I think you were getting over being sick."

John breathed deeply and appreciated how good it felt, but then he sighed and looked at Susan seriously once again.

"We don't need to worry about me; we need to worry about you, and about Steven. Susan, Steven is in very big trouble. This is way worse than I thought."

"Oh my God, what do you mean? What has he done?"

John shut his eyes and breathed deeply. He was being forced to make a difficult decision.

"Susan, I'm going to tell you about a case I had four years ago.

I never talk about my cases, but I need you to hear this. I need you to trust me completely; I need you to know what we're up against, and what I think we need to do about it."

"I do trust you John, with my life. That's why I'm here."

"It was a nineteen year old boy, Martin Douglas." John did get a slight grin thinking of this person. He was obviously fond of who ever it was. "Marty," John got a far away look in his eyes.

"Marty wanted to be in the FBI, The Federal Bureau of Investigation. Somehow for as far back as he could remember this kid just had it in his head he had to work for the FBI. He watched the TV shows, he read books, and I mean boring books. Books about every detail of evidence collection, criminal psychology, case histories. This kid didn't play baseball if you know what I mean. Some people just know what they are, and Marty has to be an FBI agent. But it was one bumpy road to get there."

John looked over at Susan. It was the middle of the night but she was wide awake hanging on every word. She had to be. John asked her, "Are you Okay to be here? Are the kids Okay?"

Susan sighed, "I have to be here, Steven's home now with the kids. I don't know what he thinks of me, but I had to get away."

"I understand," John nodded his approval.

"So this kid Marty when he graduates high school puts all his energy into getting into training for the FBI. He writes letters, he contacts his local field office, he gathers all kinds of references from teachers who are happy to oblige, but not a darn thing works. He gets no response, no interviews; it was like he was banging his head against a wall. His dream is breaking apart right before his eyes for no reason he can understand."

Susan is mesmerized by the story. She does hang on every word like her own life depends on it. It does.

John continues. "Finally one night he is in the library with a friend. He is still reading everything there is to read about FBI employment, but he actually breaks down in tears in front of her. He explains the frustration, no returned calls, no returned letters, the hopeless feeling of watching his dream die. It just so happens somebody overhears all this heartache, and Marty ends up with my business card."

Susan looked into John's eyes. She teared up, and so did John even though he couldn't help a grin. The grin got bigger.

"So here's Marty with this outrageous business card. On the one hand, he has a broken dream; on the other hand, this has to be a scam. He actually thinks perhaps he can expose me, put me away like a good FBI man, and finally somebody will listen."

John smiles deeply and shakes his head. He has deep feelings for this Marty.

"So Marty calls me. He plays it straight. He comes over here. He sat right where you're sitting. Susan, what can I tell you about chemistry? Marty starts talking, kind of wanting to get me going, but he really is hurting and I'm picking that up loud and clear. I just loved this kid. And he is trying so hard not to love me. I'm the con man he has to put away, but I'm also who I am. Honestly, somebody who just wants to get this dream on track."

There was a long silent pause as John reflected on what he had been through with Marty. Whatever had been breaking Marty's dream was a sad thing. In a way, Susan didn't want to know. Whatever was breaking her dream could be very sad. But finally she had to ask.

"So what happened? You were able to help Marty?"

John looked at Susan, and there was that mixture of love and sadness.

"Yes, I was able to help Marty, but it had to hurt him first. We dreamed together. It was Marty's father. His father sabotaged everything. He didn't relay messages, he lost letters, and he saw to it that Marty's letters did not reach their destination."

John looked at Susan with a deep sadness. "So many of us live in our little rooms, and we don't let anyone else in, even family. Marty's father had things to hide. He sure didn't need his son working for the FBI. It was horrible. It was the worst case and the best case at the same time. Being a father is what should be any man's dream. Marty's father had to learn that, and he finally did- in a dream.

That's what I do Susan. It can work, but there are no guarantees. Susan," John looked down for a long moment, but then deep in her eyes. "We need Marty."

16

Blackmail

Susan would have to trust John. She drove home. She would tell Steven she just had to get out and think. She had just wanted the party to go well for Danny. It was one too many disappointments, and she needed time to sort it all out. In the mean time she knew John would contact Marty, the FBI. Steven was in some kind of trouble, and it had to do with a mysterious news van John had spotted in front of his house. She had to wonder if her whole family was in danger. She had to wonder what was going on, and she had to wonder if there was any hope left for her dream.

John unlocked his file cabinet and pulled out Marty's chart. He looked at the display on his cell phone, three AM. "Wish this could wait," he muttered. Sebastian made a brief purring sound. John dialed Marty's cell number.

"Hello John, is that you?" The FBI man had caller ID.

"Marty, yes it's me. How's the FBI life?"

"John Dreamer, three AM, this must be good. Hey buddy, I'm always here for you. Have you finally decided to help me catch the bad guys?"

For a while Marty had been rather relentless in his attempts to get John to use his gifts to help the FBI in their investigations. "There's too much suffering going on, and it has to be stopped. We need you. I need you." Marty had done his best to try to convince John his senses could be put to better use. But John always had the same answer. "You catch the bad guys, I fix broken dreams. We do what we are."

"John it is so good to hear your voice. I've been real worried about you. I know this cancer thing has got to be such a nightmare. I wish we'd be in touch more. How are you anyway?"

"Well, I think the powers that be have decided to keep me around. I could call it a miracle, but every day is a miracle in my book."

"I'm so glad to hear you're alright, but I bet you didn't just call to chat at three AM."

"Brilliant deduction Watson," John joked. "Marty I really do need your help. I just may help you catch the bad guys, or gals, but I need you to help me make sure the right folks get caught."

"My ThinkPad is booted up, what have you got?"

"Richard's Realty."

"Okay give me a minute. You know we can't be having this conversation."

"That works both ways Marty. I really care about my case."

"Understood. Here we go, it's coming up now. Oh my God. Holy shit John. We've got an eight month investigation, so far looks like three million dollars. People are buying houses that have no business buying houses. Blackmail, extortion, geez you don't fool around. I can't believe this. I'd say we could certainly use your help Dreamer. If you've got something on Steven Richards I'm all ears, this is really big John."

"That's just what I was afraid of. Marty, I need you to trust me on this, and I need a little time. Forty eight hours maybe. I don't think it's Steven Richards. It's his assistant Barbara Hayes. I think she's blackmailing him too, I don't know what for. But it gets better. Marty, Steven's wife Susan is about to be blackmailed. We can see this coming and use her to take this whole thing down."

"Susan Richards is about to be blackmailed, for what?"

"For having an affair."

"With who?"

John shook his head, he had to say it. "With me."

There was a long silence as Marty took this all in. Finally John broke it, "Sebastian got your tongue?"

"So you're helping Susan."

"Yes, and last night we were filmed by a Bayside News 7 van, I have a partial, 417. I think the driver's name is Mark. I grabbed the door handle; I punched the left rear quarter panel. I think I made a dent. They're using this news van. The camera equipment is probably top of the line, everything they need to catch people at their worst."

"John I hear you. I'm with you on this, believe me. I'll do all I can, but you have to know this is Richard's Realty, not Hayes Realty. Don't be so sure we can save Steven on this one."

"First things first. Susan is going to be getting a package. I don't know what Barbara will try to pull with this. She may look for money. She seems to want Steven for herself. She controls him terribly. We need to meet with Susan and explain what to do with her package when it arrives. I didn't tell her yet what was going down. Then Marty, I need to get Steven in a dream and get him out from Barbara's clutches. He will have to come clean about whatever he knows. I know he's got to end it, or it ends him. He's got a beautiful family. His wife deserves all we can do for her."

"Oh boy John. You are the dreamer. I hope to God you get through this alright. I know what you did for me. I'll never bet against you. Get some sleep. I'll pick you up at nine AM sharp tomorrow morning, I mean this morning. I've got to get into the office and start explaining to the agents working the Richard's Realty case what we have going on. I hope we can buy you the time you need. Don't be so sure. Five hours from now. I mean it, get some sleep. I think you'll like my car. Sorry we have to skip church, but God better help you on this one buddy, and we have a day before Monday starts a new week. We've got to plan this out thoroughly. Go to sleep."

"Thank you Marty. Good to be talking with you again. Wish it didn't have to be under these circumstances. See you at nine, we'll right the wrongs."

John got under his tightly tucked covers. Sebastian jumped on the bed and purred beside him.

"I guess I've really got to earn my pay buddy," John shared his thoughts with the old kitty. Then, as he so often did, he spoke to Kari.

"Wherever you are, this looks like a rough and rocky road ahead of me. I don't know if I could do it without a dream. You are my dream, and with everything I have I'm giving this my best shot."

John remembered ever so briefly his fleeting thought of Susan at the waterfall.

"Perhaps a clue." John tried to put the thoughts out of his head. Lovers and broken dreams were mixing his thoughts. He had to focus. This case was taking on a life of its own. The FBI had a file on Richard's Realty, and things were looking very bad indeed. Steven had to know the details of his home sales. How much did he know about Barbara's magic? What wall of fear could Barbara create that kept Steven from seeing the truth?

"We're going to find out."

17

Broken Sleep

John tucked the sheet tight, force of habit, but one that was
conductive for dreams. He lay there in his bed and felt the soreness
in his left hand. He had held the door handle of that van very
tightly, and it yanked away until he couldn't hold it anymore.
Then he had punched the van. The soreness in his hand was the
connection to that van, and to Mark. He only thought about
getting some sleep, but it wasn't long before another important
dream.

John found himself in the back seat of a dark blue Toyota
Camry. It was new, and pretty fancy. Barbara was driving. She
couldn't know John was behind her. She was following behind
an older black Ford Bronco. It was a dream, but John was in
that state where he knew it. He breathed deeply and felt his
stillness and invisibility. This was Barbara's recent past. She was
following Mark. Ahead of Mark was a small yellow school bus.
It approached Bayside Elementary School. John watched the kids
getting out. One of the kids was Danny Richards. John sat up
intently. The bus took off, and Mark followed it. Barbara kept
up, but did leave more and more distance. John wondered what
was going on, and if Barbara and Mark were together on this or
not. Barbara left more and more distance. If she was following

Mark she might lose him, but Mark stayed very close behind the school bus.

Finally going down a side street more out in the country the bus pulled into the driveway of an ordinary residential house. The driveway was on the right side of this house. A tall clump of hedges concealed the right side of the bus. The driver got out of the bus and went up to the door of the house. A woman let him in. Being in a dream, John just knew what this was about. The bus had picked up her child earlier, now the driver was back for some fun with mom.

Barbara stayed pretty far back from this whole scene, but she got out a fancy camcorder. At first John thought she would be trying to blackmail the bus driver, or the child's mother. But what happened next was beyond his reckoning. Mark had parked to the right of the driveway, on the other side of the hedges. Barbara put her camcorder on him as he got out of the Bronco.

"It's not that I don't love you and appreciate your help Mark. I need Steven shaken up now. But it never hurts to have insurance. Let's hope I never need to use it."

John was totally bewildered, but what he saw next blew him away. Mark quickly got a tire iron out of the back seat of his Bronco. He slipped between the bus and the hedges, and loosened the lug nuts on the right rear tire of the bus. This was Danny's school bus. Mark had been responsible for that accident. Susan had caught the whole thing on her camcorder, though she had put him up to it.

The next thing he knew John was in Barbara's house. She hung up her coat, poured herself a drink, and took the tape out of her camcorder and played it over her flat screen video monitor. The picture was flawless. Mark's crime was clearly in focus, his face unmistakable. "Bingo," Barbara muttered. She put the film cartridge in a special cartridge file along one wall of her study.

Suddenly John was in the bus with Danny. The kids were so

happy to be going home, but then the bus lost control, everybody screamed. John screamed too as he woke up.

He struggled to get out from his tightly wrapped covers. He was almost out of breath and his heart was pounding. "These people will stop at nothing," He thought to himself. "Nobody is safe. This keeps getting worse, and we're running out of time."

18

9AM

John stepped out his front door. The sun shined directly in his eyes. He held it back with his right hand. He heard the sound of an approaching car. He glanced at his hand full of sunshine and briefly made a fist as if he held the power of the sun in his hand. Sebastian watched from his window.

"Wish us luck," John pleaded with his great cat.

There was a honk. John smiled and shook his head. Marty set off a brief siren. It was a glistening black Lincoln Town car. Marty was in a dark blue suit, dark shades, but a bright smile. What a piece of work.

"Need a lift?"

"To church?"

Marty got out and gave John a bear hug. "Hey man, you are looking good. I've never seen you look this good. What happened?" Marty was shocked.

"A woman. What else?" John appeared caught.

"Do tell." Marty was all ears now.

"That will really have to wait. Honest to God, forget I said anything. I'm dreaming. Marty, I'm really afraid of what is happening with my case. I had another dream about it last night. It is evil Marty. It is freaking me out. I don't know if I can stick with this."

"John, I know you are not cut out for evil. Hang in there, I am. I deal with this machine every single day. That's what it is John, a dam machine. If you think flesh and blood for a minute you're dead. You must have seen something horrible. Well welcome to my world. But John, I have to fight the good fight. Once in a while we really push it back. That's what keeps me going. We do stop the bad guys. If we can play our cards straight, just once in a while, we put them away. We protect and serve, as the police say."

"Thank you for being here for me Marty. Where are we going?"

"Not far, the local field office. A team of agents is working the Richard's Realty case. We're going to have a meeting. I'm sorry it may be a tough crowd for you, but in this evil business we can't play games. Everything has to come out. The stakes are too high. You have to tell us everything you know."

"Yeah Marty, but your colleagues are not going to appreciate listening to dreams. They will think you are a nut case, and maybe think I should be put away."

"John, I know this is going to put you on the suspect list with the worst of them, but like you taught me- the truth is what matters. Everybody has to know what it is. You just tell it like it is. You don't have to prove anything, we do."

Marty drove that awesome car into the parking lot of a beautiful office building, and up to a parking spot with a sign that said, "Marty."

Marty took off his shades and gave John an almost evil grin.

"I should have charged you double," John joked.

"Don't forget, your bad dream last night is my day to day business. I earn this."

"No argument there."

They walked to the building. Marty typed a code and stuck his hand in a small opening. The door buzzed and he opened it.

John followed Marty through the building, up an elevator to

the 4th floor, down a long hallway to a door. FBI Bayside Field Office. John took a deep breath. This was some case.

"Good morning everybody," Marty spoke like he was some star of the show. "I'm sorry to bring you in here on a Sunday, but evidence pops up on its own schedule. This is my friend John Dreamer. I've told you a little bit about him. He is a type of counselor who has happened to be working with Steven Richard's wife Susan. In that capacity he has been exposed to aspects of the case you have been working on. John," Marty spoke to John and began to introduce the agents, "This is Laurie, Robert, David, and Kyle."

John shook hands with each agent and looked into their eyes for understanding.

"I'm very pleased to meet Marty's colleagues."

David looked very serious, and was an obvious authority in this group. John felt that right away. But this would not be as difficult as John feared.

David spoke first. "Mr. Dreamer, Marty's probably told me more than he has the others about you. I have some things I want to say. I'm betting you have a lot of apprehension about meeting with us this morning. But you know it's the right thing to do. There are some very serious issues going on here. Not only blackmail, but attempted murder. Emotions can run wild. I want you to know we appreciate it when citizens step forward. It can make or break a case. I don't know all about the counseling you do, or if it has some psychic component to it, but ever since the development of psychological profiling the bureau has been more receptive to people's impressions and feelings. Do I understand correctly that you pick up on that sort of thing? Impressions? Feelings?"

John was quickly feeling better. These were the good guys. Marty and the Bureau were what he needed. He had felt some temptation each time Marty had begged him to get involved with cases. He introduced himself to this gathering.

"Yes, I am a counselor who you could say profiles. I watch, take notes, and get impressions of the people around me, and around my clients. We have common ground in our trust of Marty. Thank you David for your kind words. I did the right thing calling Marty. My client is Susan Richards, the wife of Steven Richards. My actions have been on her behalf with an interest in healing their marriage. I understand your suspicions of Steven Richards, but I do believe in the fundamental goodness of the Richards family, and I hold out hope for their marriage."

David spoke up again. He wasn't angry, just firm and concerned.

"Mr. Dreamer, over the past eight months three realty companies have come forward to report clients who were well bonded to these companies and in the final stages of purchasing houses when they all of a sudden bought from Richard's Realty. It was not only a rude break from these realty companies which was out of character. These particular clients bought houses from Richard's Realty which were clearly out of their established price ranges. It was enough of a shock that the Realtors came to us.

John nodded his head in approval, and spoke up well.

"I very much understand. I went house hunting with Steven Richards and his associate Barbara. I did it more to learn of Steven Richards and his life, I wasn't interested in a house purchase. What I encountered was a pathetic man completely controlled by his associate. Mr. Richards mentioned to me that Barbara could make a sale like magic. Magic was the word he used. Last night Susan Richards came to my home distraught over Steven's failure to honor a promise to their son. As Susan and I were talking I noticed a Bayside News 7 van outside my home. I rushed outside, but as soon as the operator realized I saw the van he bolted out of there. I'm sure he was filming Susan and me, and I'm sure Susan will be blackmailed and accused of having an affair with me because of the actions of that van driver. I believe his name is Mark. I grabbed the driver's side door handle but couldn't get in.

I also punched the driver's side rear quarter panel. I got a partial plate number, 417."

Kyle spoke up this time. "We are just at the stage in this investigation where we will begin to question the home buyers. We plan on going in tough, no games, and getting answers. We plan on showing them they will have more to fear from us than Richard's Realty."

John pleaded. "I believe Barbara Hayes, Steven's associate, is behind any blackmail that is going on. I believe she is blackmailing Steven to control him. As I said to Marty, she is about to blackmail Susan Richards and you can catch her in the act here. But there's more I haven't told you. I can't tell you how I get this information. I can only tell you what I know. Barbara followed Mark a few weeks ago. She was driving a blue Toyota Camry; he was driving a black Ford Bronco. Mark was following a school bus. When that school bus parked and the driver left, Mark got a tire iron out of the back of his car and loosened the lug nuts on the right rear tire of the bus. Barbara filmed the whole thing. The proof of this is in a film cartridge in a file in Barbara's study. It is as good as a surveillance camera, or better. Barbara made that tape as an insurance policy in case Mark got out of line. She could threaten him with that film. The tire came off that bus in an accident, and Steven Richard's son was on the bus at that time. He was slightly injured, but it could have been so much worse, and everybody knows that.

David was shocked, and took the floor. "John, we are investigating that bus accident. We do know it was no accident. But how can you give us that kind of information and not be willing to reveal how you got it?"

John shook his head. He knew it was very problematic. He spoke softly. "I don't get this information, it comes to me."

David was serious as he should be. "We have no reason to believe you, no witnesses; we can't get a warrant on any of this."

Marty spoke now. "If John says it, I believe it. In fact, I'd stake my life on it. So we know what's up. Barbara Hayes and some guy Mark, we need to investigate who has access to Bayside News 7 Vans, these two are blackmailers, and they've got something on Steven Richards so they control him. We need to give John time to get to the bottom of what Barbara has on Steven, and then we can track Barbara's blackmailing Susan. Then we can get our warrants and proof and convictions."

David stood up. He was shaking his head in a futile disgust. "This is getting out of hand. We have policies and procedures, strict guidelines and laws we must follow. No matter how we may wish John has some way of getting information by magic, we are getting nowhere."

Marty shook his head too, but with a cocky grin. David didn't appreciate it. John seemed to dread it, but finally Marty just turned to John and said, "Show him."

David said, "Show me what?"

John just kind of smiled and shrugged his head. "Okay, David, give me your hand."

David extended his hand. John took it and held it a minute looking into David's eyes. Then John sat back down, took out his notebook and wrote something down. John looked at Marty and raised his eyebrows. Marty nodded. John handed the notebook to David. David looked at what was written and his jaw could have just dropped to the floor. John had written David's personal user name and password to get in to all the FBI computer files. There was no way to describe the look on David's face as he stared at John.

John blurted out, "I'll never tell."

David spoke up to the whole group. "We need to investigate who has access to Bayside News 7 vans. Find out who this Mark character is and put 24 hour surveillance on Mark and Barbara. John you have 48 hours to find out what Barbara has on Steven. We will meet back here Wednesday night at 8PM with Susan and

Steven and play out Barbara's blackmail scheme against Susan. Any questions?"

John mingled with the agents for a few minutes after the meeting. At one point Marty noticed John and Laurie having a discussion and looking in his direction. John was nodding his head. The two of them shared a brief laugh. Marty finally walked over to them.

"Anybody need a ride home?" He asked.

"In that fancy car I'll take it," John smiled. He was very glad things had gone as well as they did, though he didn't understand how his senses could be so strong.

19

Talk Of Dreams

Back in Marty's Lincoln John was very quiet. Things were a bit awkward briefly, but Marty broke the silence.

"I bet I know what's bothering you?"

"You mean what's at the top of the list?"

"Yes. You need to dream again. John, it was the experience of a lifetime to dream with you, but I know it was also horrible. I guess it always is, isn't it?"

"Horrible is the word. I'm sorry. I could have died when we discovered the part your father played in your troubles. It is always a nightmare."

"But John, you know such good comes out of it. I got my father back. He paid the price; he chose to be my father when push came to shove."

John breathed hard. He looked Marty in the eye, and then lightened up.

"That was some meeting. Show him?" John shook his head. "Just what did you think I could show him?"

Marty chuckled, "Well Jesus Christ you sure showed him something. I don't suppose you'd care to tell me what?"

"That wouldn't be proper. I can't believe I did that myself. I don't know if it is my health or what. I'm different Marty. It scares me. The senses are stronger. I seem to be in some kind of amazing remission, or cured."

"What about this girl you mentioned?" Marty was taking aim at John. "Is she the cure all? Can I be best man?"

John got a look on his face Marty could read like a billboard.

"Oh buddy, you've got it bad now."

John sat up and glared at Marty, but all with love. "I shouldn't have said anything. I'm dreaming. When I find the girl of my dreams you will be one of the first to know."

"Not the first? You know what that tells me?"

John looked up at the car roof. "What?"

"John, you're going to find her."

John got that far away look in his eyes again. He sat quietly and shook his head. As difficult as so much had been in his life, he had never felt such hope. Even the longing for her was such a beautiful gift. To feel what every poet has felt, even if he couldn't find the words. He could see Kari's face, and he really couldn't stop seeing it.

"Marty I really appreciate your help. This blackmail business is horrible. I wish it didn't touch the life of anyone as precious as Susan Richards, or her children. I don't know where Steven fits in all of this, but it is no place of honor."

"You heard David, and Kyle. We're closing in John. The likes of Barbara and Mark don't stop until we stop them, and we will. You have given us a great boost in this investigation John. I always wanted you by my side. Is the car good enough for you?"

John and Marty both laughed, and it felt so good to let some of the tension go.

"It will do."

John's cell phone rang.

"It's Susan Richards." John's demeanor changed. He was gentle yet concerned.

"Hi Susan. How are you?"

"Worried about you. I know you hurt your hand last night, and you were so upset. How are you doing?"

"I'm Okay Susan, and I'm getting us the help we need. I've had to do it Susan. I'm not saying it is Steven, but Richard's Realty is in serious trouble. What we saw last night is part of it. I'm glad you called, we need to talk. I'm in the car with Marty now. We've had a meeting at the FBI field office. Susan listen to me. That van last night was catching us together. You are going to get a package Susan, with photos of us. Who ever sends the photos will threaten to show them to Steven. They think you and I are having an affair. They catch things like this on film with that van, and blackmail people. You've got to trust me and keep quiet. I'm afraid people are being blackmailed to buy houses from Richard's Realty."

"Oh my God John." Susan wept over the phone.

"Susan, I don't know what part Steven plays in all this. I'm holding out hope that he is a good man. He is afraid, and maybe he is being blackmailed like you will be. You know we did nothing wrong, but those photos may look bad."

"What could anyone want from me?" Susan cried out.

"Don't open the package when it arrives. Try not to handle it. Call me and I'll get Marty and we'll come and help you. We'll need evidence from the package, and to see what it is about."

"I don't want to know."

"We will get through this Susan. Remember what this is really all about Susan. It is about a broken dream. Give Steven vitamins and tuck him in tight. I'm going to work on this tomorrow night. Don't be afraid Susan. You need to trust me. This is all about seeing if we can fix a beautiful dream for a beautiful family. Never forget you are a beautiful person with a beautiful dream. It is worth whatever we can do. We have to try."

"Are you sure you're Okay?"

John shook his head. Susan was worried about him at a time like this.

"I'm Okay Susan. We've got good people on our side. Go easy on yourself, take it easy. Sweet dreams."

"Okay, talk to you soon. Bye."

John shut the phone. He stared at it, then looked at Marty. They pulled up to John's apartment and Marty stopped the car.

Marty reached out his hand, John took it. "You're a good man John Dreamer. Get some rest. You've got a big week ahead of you. I'm always just a phone call away. I always told you we make a good team. We're going to catch us some bad guys."

"And gals," John added.

"Yes sir. I'll be in touch."

John sat there for a minute still taking in the experience of being in such a car. "This is some set of wheels Mr. Douglas. You are doing pretty well for yourself I must say."

"I get by," Marty grinned.

"Any lady friends for you?"

"Maybe I'm a slow learner in that department."

"Agent Laurie was pretty cute."

"Do you know something I don't?"

John pointed his finger at Marty in a make shift gun. "Bingo."

John got out, shook his head once more at the fancy car, and shut the door. He waved, and Marty made a brief sound with the siren in his car as he drove off.

John grinned. "Show off." He watched the car until it disappeared out of view. Then he heard another motor. He looked up in the window and saw Sebastian looking down on the world, seeing to it that all is well.

"You're in luck fella; I'm in the mood to spoil you rotten today. Somebody has to have a good day, and you are the chosen one. A fresh can of Fancy Feast and a fine brushing. What do you say? I just have to make a quick phone call."

20

Planning

Susan paced back and forth through the house. Danny and Caitlin were watching cartoons. Steven had run out on some errands but did say he would be back soon. Maybe it wasn't work this time. Susan trembled in fear thinking of everything John had said. Her whole life and that of her children hung in the balance. She questioned herself as she always did. Should she ever have called John? Were things that bad? Maybe she would be wreaking everything for Steven. Susan had lots of practice blaming herself for everything and defending Steven.

But she had only to look at some of the left-over party favors to know that things were that bad. She couldn't have a birthday party for Danny without heartache. This life was not what she had dreamed. She took out one of her photo albums. She sat down in a big recliner. It was the chair where Steven used to sit and read stories to the family almost every night. This photo album had a picture of Steven at story time. He looked so happy. It was a shock to see. Steven had not looked that happy in a long time. Whatever had caused their dream to fade away was hurting Steven as well as everybody else. It actually brought Susan some hope to think she wasn't hurting alone. Steven was hurting too, but he was keeping it all from her. He always said he had nothing to hide, that he had not cheated, that he loved his family more then anything. But his life was way different now than it was in this photo album she held. The pictures in that album were of the dream that was. She loved these photo albums. It was tangible proof she had not been crazy. This had been a beautiful dream. How could anything have ruined it?

There was more. One picture showed Danny riding on Steven's shoulders, his hands wrapped around Steve's forehead. Susan looked at that picture. Danny was absolutely beaming from ear to ear. Susan put her hand to her mouth. The flood of tears came and there was nothing she could do about it. "Oh my God," she whispered. Time was a very precious thing. Somehow Susan had always known that, and like her own mother she was very intent on capturing it on film and honoring it as best she could. It was so difficult now to see Danny that happy. The precious gift of time was being wasted. For all the fear she felt there was also the resolution that things had to change. She would face that for her and her children.

John looked over all his notes as Sebastian munched away on Fancy Feast. He looked up from his reading to see it was ten minutes past four PM in the afternoon. He grabbed the phone.

"Hello," came the beautiful voice on the other end.

"Helen its John. I need to talk to you."

"Well get here by five PM and we can talk over some fine cooking. If you could smell it over the phone I wouldn't have to ask."

"I'm on my way, thanks."

There was quite a spring in his steps as he leaped out his front door.

"Better see if this family knows how to cook."

John stopped dead in his tracks with that thought. He almost couldn't breathe. He sat down on his front steps. Helen was having him over for dinner. It made everything seem real, and the reality was hitting home. Helen had been the most special nurse he could ever hope for, and that relationship was changing.

It should be for the better, but John was not immune to the fear of change. Not when the change can be this big. So much was riding on him. The Susan Richard's case would have been stress enough, but with all he felt for Helen he couldn't bear the thought he might fail to find her daughter. With all that had happened he felt that he couldn't fail. But how could he succeed? This was too good to be true.

"Have some faith." He got up and tried to shake the emotions from his mind in order to be able to function. He had to lighten up. He breathed in the fresh air. It was time to go smell some great home cooking.

As soon as he parked the car John saw Helen at the front door waving him in.

"Right on time. Does this smell good enough for you?"

John was close to choked up. "Oh my God do I dare get used to this?"

"If Kari can't make it like this yet she will when I'm through with her."

The two of them embraced in a warm hug, but with the mention of Kari the magnitude of the dream became all encompassing. There was a fairly long silence. But between such decent people silence was friendly. The love and trust in the room was equal to the awesome smell of pork chops, garden green beans, and garden grown potatoes.

"Garden fresh is the only way to eat like this John."

John shook his head. "I have to pinch myself to be sure this isn't a dream here."

Helen knew they had some serious discussion coming. "So John, just how are you feeling?"

"I'm feeling good Helen. I don't know if I've ever felt this good. I've been sick for so long I suppose just normal would feel awesome to me, but I do suspect this is better than normal. I'm actually frightened. It was an incredible dream, God it is almost too much to bear to see Kari. She knew I was sick, more than I did. She gave me that medicine."

"Fusheeswa," Helen beamed as she looked at her John.

"You said it, and I'm content to let you say it. So what is it anyway?"

Helen got a far away look in her eye. "John, by the grace of God, I've got to let Kari tell you that, you best hear it from her."

John looked at Helen very seriously, "It is worth waiting for."

With nothing said they both knew this was miracle talk. They had made miracles happen, but it never got easier or less astounding. It didn't make faith easier.

John spoke up. "Helen, I need to do a dream tomorrow night. This case is pushing me. I am so very sorry this is such short notice, but an FBI investigation is coming down on Richard's Realty. Susan Richards could lose everything. She might anyway, but there is something so beautiful about her dream. The Richard's family was a dream family. At times I feel there is some connection to Kari in this case. Maybe it is just Susan's love, but it feels like something more. I have to dream into Steven's nightmare and bring him out of it, but I'm worried."

"Worried about what?" Helen asked.

"If I can still do this. These incredible dreams, for me I have felt perhaps they were some side effect or byproduct of my illness. The way a tumor might affect the brain. I've wondered from the beginning where my illness fit in this picture. It seemed certain your medication was what pushed this over the top. I have no expectation I could do this without chemotherapy, your special chemotherapy. But I don't feel like I'm ill. We don't know about my condition. Helen, the sensitivity has been unbelievable. I've needed it to make progress in this case, but it has never worked so well."

"You mean how you sense things around you or pick up thoughts?"

"Oh Helen, honest to God, I had to get through to a tough

crowd at the FBI field office, I took a leader of the group by the hand, read him like a book, and wrote down his user name and password for the FBI data base."

Helen burst out laughing. John shook his head because this was so darn serious, but there was no denying a humorous element.

John gave Helen a look. "It's not funny."

"Oh John I'm sorry, but in a way I'm not. You know we have both been scared to freaking death the whole time over this dream business and your health. But after our visit to the church I've done some real soul searching. I know I've got to put this in God's hands. I've prayed for my daughter everyday." She looked at John. "And I pray for you everyday. Maybe before this year is up I can get you both in with one prayer."

John looked down and fell silent. Helen continued to speak.

"John there's more. I've been thinking a lot about this too. Dr. Bernard is a great support to me. He told me not to bet against you when we had your test results as a death sentence staring us in the face. I'm sure he would be glad to be right even if he can't believe it himself. Come in to the office early tomorrow afternoon. I'm sure Dr. Bernard will back us and write the prescriptions for all the tests we need to put you through. We need fresh results. Dr. Bernard watched you come in to the office and pass out nearly dead. Tomorrow you will walk into the office looking so handsome the nurses won't be able to get their jobs done. Everybody is going to want an answer. God forgive me but I've got one. You went to another nurse. I forgive you John. Must have been some hell of a nurse."

John shook his head in astonishment. "I'll say."

"John, we may want to put in a good word for that nurse. Bayside might just be a good place for her to work in this area."

"Now who is the dreamer?" John smiled.

"John I am a very good nurse. It's because I'm so old I've seen it all. You don't look sick...at all. I'm not sure what part my help plays in your dreaming, but I'll tell Dr. Bernard I need to stay late as I so often do. We'll get our room in the office again for dreaming. What I do with your IV is very natural, but partly what I focus on is natural sedation and keeping you on oxygen. I have not told you all the thought I put into this before. You have to sleep through the whole dream. These dreams are tough on you. It makes for very restless sleep and broken breaths. The oxygen and sedatives keep you on an even keel through them. I want you on the monitors for my own peace of mind. If something starts to go south I can't waste a moment. I was always worried because you were so frail. Now maybe I'll have to strap you in."

John had a renewed feeling about just what good hands he was in. "God bless you Helen. We really are a team. And we are making the most of the hands we are dealt. I so hope we can keep the Richard's family intact. And I swear to you with all that I am I will be living to bring Kari to you, where she belongs."

"Now don't get cold feet Mr. Dreamer. Seems to me from the look I have seen on your face Kari belongs with you. You get her here for sure, but you better be ready for anything."

"You drive a hard bargain. This time I'll look forward to all those blasted medical tests. I do feel very well. My perceptions have never been so strong, and I'm getting a strong one now. You have some kind of dessert, don't you?"

21

An Examined Life

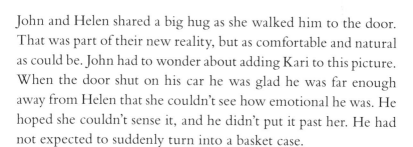

John and Helen shared a big hug as she walked him to the door. That was part of their new reality, but as comfortable and natural as could be. John had to wonder about adding Kari to this picture. When the door shut on his car he was glad he was far enough away from Helen that she couldn't see how emotional he was. He hoped she couldn't sense it, and he didn't put it past her. He had not expected to suddenly turn into a basket case.

He prayed through his tears, to Kari. "Well now look what's happened. I'm the luckiest person in the world to know your mother. If I could have ever had a wish to be able to thank her for all her care over the years." He had to wipe his face and blow his nose.

"Where ever you are in this world I am sending you all the love a heart can hold. You just hang in there, and help me if you can."

John took the scenic route home. The gazebo haunted him enough that he stopped for a closer look. There were no signs forbidding a night time visit. The lights around the pond made this a perfect romantic spot. John thought perhaps he shouldn't push his emotions any further, but fresh air was calming, as was the quacking sounds from the water. He climbed up the stairs into the gazebo and looked down on the water. A mother duck with four babies was swimming by. John looked around the empty gazebo and imagined showing this to Kari. He didn't know if he could do it. He had spent years alone. It wouldn't be fair to get involved with anyone since he had a terminal illness. But Kari knew him better than he knew himself. Deep down he did know how much love was in his heart. If love was what mattered maybe he wasn't such a bad catch.

He called out to Kari, "You're not the only one who can find a beautiful spot young lady."

A couple was walking toward the gazebo and John hoped they didn't hear him talking to his imaginary friend. He better get home and let this couple live their dream come true. He could only hope and pray his day would come.

He drove off in the night. The couple actually passed by the gazebo this time, just enjoying their walk. But the gazebo had not been empty. Up on one of the beams supporting the roof of the gazebo sat a little owl who had watched over John and his prayers. Without a sound, it launched itself into the night.

There were no dreams that night. Perhaps it was to conserve energy. John was up early and reviewed all his notes as Sebastian enjoyed a big breakfast.

"Tonight's the big night buddy. Wish me lots of luck."

Sebastian let out a typical cat sound and pushed his head against one of John's hands. "Thanks, now I'm sure to succeed."

John looked over all his notes again. It was quite an accumulation by now. He needed to get everything together in his mind and keep mindful of the big picture. There were major pieces missing. He would need to find them and find where they fit. He really never could feel prepared enough, but if he was tested on this material he would pass. It also passed the time before his appointment.

John walked to Bayside. He needed the calming effect of a long walk. Helen could drive him home if all went well. He had ideas about how to handle Steven if the opportunity presented itself. John faced stress over the dream, and equal stress over the medical tests concerning his condition. He thought about all the stress Susan must be feeling. There certainly is enough to go around. With a dream to live for John had to take one step at a time, which is all anybody can do.

"Here goes," John said to himself as he walked through the revolving doors of Bayside Medical Center. His walk was strong. He consciously felt the strength of his breath, the spring in his step. Could his health actually be as good as he suspected it was? He paused at the chapel, stood there for a moment thinking of all the times he had spent in there praying and wondering. He was early enough to take a moment inside and reflect on all that had happened over the years, and especially what he faced now. The only prayer to say was actually very simple. "I'm in your hands."

John looked down as he walked, deep in thought as he approached the office of Dr. Gary Bernard. So many times, over the years he had walked through this door, but always it was hoping to receive a miracle. Now he was hoping to give one. Everyday with every breath he had given thanks for one more chance to be in the game. One couldn't deny that life was an amazing adventure. But John and Helen had been dealing with the impossible. With connections they couldn't explain, with powers they couldn't possess. How could they explain John's health?

"There's my John," Helen beamed. Their eyes locked in a magical glance with both of them feeling a tad giddy. They didn't realize Dr. Bernard saw them in this moment.

"Good afternoon Helen. I'm here for a major check up, and I must confess I envy myself for the way I feel. I said a prayer at the Chapel, nothing for granted here."

"Have some faith, good to hear. I have to tell you Dr. Bernard was surprised to see you on the schedule. Rather glad, but surprised. This is going to test his heart John. Go easy on him."

John laughed and shook his head. "I really can't believe this."

"Well first things first." Helen took John in one of the exam rooms along with his chart. It had to be the biggest chart in Bayside. She took his vital signs and started shaking her head too. "Temperature ninety eight point six, blood pressure one hundred twenty over sixty five, weight one hundred forty, up from one hundred twenty five a month ago. Her laughter had a low tone that built up as she spoke, "Boy I want to be a fly on this wall Mr. Dreamer. How are you going to explain this, my cooking?"

"Hey I'm the patient here. I'm looking for answers, not giving them."

"Well the doctor will be in shortly. Help yourself to a magazine John." She kissed him on the cheek, and wished him serious good luck.

John sat there in the exam room and pondered everything. This adventure sure had a dream like quality. It often felt like he was living a dream, and it was really a dream come true to be living at all after so many close calls. As the minutes ticked by he thought about this great hospital. It really could be a place for Kari to work. No doubt she was an awesome nurse, but John must be the only person on the planet to receive...Fusheeswa, whatever that was. Whatever it all could mean that must be reserved just for him. Would he ever find out what it was all about? Even Helen wouldn't tell. But she knew, and that was enough.

John watched the clock on the wall. All good doctors have to keep their patients waiting. It must be some secret rule. Twenty minutes had gone by. He would be ready when it came time for a urine sample. Finally a knock, and in came Dr. Bernard.

"John Dreamer, very good to see you here again." Dr. Bernard was warm and friendly, but there was no doubt John was a shocking sight to this medical professional who had not seen it all until today.

"Good to be here I must say," John replied.

John was sitting on the exam table. Dr. Bernard sat on his stool rolled over to his desk. He kept looking at John, and back in the chart, flipping the pages, his lips got tight. "John strip down, you know you certainly need a thorough exam. This is quite a diagnosis we have been dealing with through the years."

John complied.

After twenty minutes of waiting in this exam room John started to look at the clock as Dr. Bernard kept reading through his chart. John sensed some fear. The chart was manageable, black and white, and easy to read. What was he looking at?

Dr. Bernard gave John a thorough exam as he had so often done before. He was a good doctor, and not so quick to let the machines figure it all out. He listened to John's heart very intently. He had John breathe deeply as he listened, and kept listening. Dr. Bernard was studying John like he was going to have to answer for this. It seemed he shined a light in John's eyes an especially long time. He had John lie down and he felt what must have been every organ of his body.

"Well," one quick word was all Dr. Bernard spoke, but then he was back at John's chart flipping though all the pages over and over. John had a quick flash of remembering Kari saying to him, "You're not that good." The expression on his face when he remembered Kari must have revealed something. Dr. Bernard finally struggled for some words.

He cleared his throat. "John Dreamer, we have been working with you for five years and I've never seen you like this. I want every test in the book over again. John this looks very good. I'm happy, don't get me wrong please, but we take our medical care very seriously. You don't appear to be in any remission. You don't look like you ever had an illness. I know there is something going on between you and Helen. I mean nothing bad; they don't get any better than Helen. But if she pushed the envelope for you I want you to come clean. I'm a doctor. Healing people is what this is all about, and I want to know how you can appear this well. If the tests back this up...John you can't expect us to just smile and say congratulations here."

John sat up and looked into his doctor's eyes. "Dr. Bernard, I can't ever tell you how much the care you and Helen have given me has meant to me. It is not just medical care, you care. I care about people too. I know something happened to me. If I could give you some explanation for what has happened I would do that, but I honestly don't know. Since you last examined me I have had Helen's cooking, and I have fallen in love. I'm inclined to want to pin this on one or both of those experiences. I know that is not in the world of medical sense. Prayers have been said too. You don't see a hospital without a chapel. Maybe what I can say is if you want to heal people, use every tool in the box."

Dr. Bernard shook John's hand. "I will pray the lab work looks as good as my physical exam. You may just be an advertisement for our chapel."

22

Tricks Of The Trade

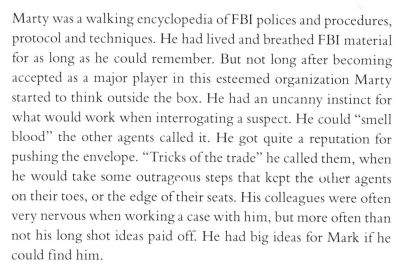

Marty was a walking encyclopedia of FBI polices and procedures, protocol and techniques. He had lived and breathed FBI material for as long as he could remember. But not long after becoming accepted as a major player in this esteemed organization Marty started to think outside the box. He had an uncanny instinct for what would work when interrogating a suspect. He could "smell blood" the other agents called it. He got quite a reputation for pushing the envelope. "Tricks of the trade" he called them, when he would take some outrageous steps that kept the other agents on their toes, or the edge of their seats. His colleagues were often very nervous when working a case with him, but more often than not his long shot ideas paid off. He had big ideas for Mark if he could find him.

The people of Bayside News 7 noticed when that sleek Lincoln Town car pulled into their parking lot followed by other cars and a black van with no markings on it. Marty and another agent got out of the town car. Two agents got out of one of the other cars. Nobody got out of the black van. All of the agents were wearing wires. The van could pick up everything and record even a man's breath. Marty was calling the shots on this one.

Marty approached the main desk with the other agents behind him. He flashed his FBI badge and asked to speak with someone in management. Everybody jumped to attention and he was promptly escorted into a plush office where the CEO of News 7 was very welcoming.

"Good morning, I'm James Duncan. How can I be of help to you gentleman?"

"Good morning Mr. Duncan, my name is Martin Douglas, this is Agent Dawson, Marty and Robert will be fine. We're here because we have reason to believe one of your employees is involved in serious criminal activities and that he uses one of your Bayside News 7 vans. This past Saturday night a witness reported seeing one of your vans outside his residence. It appeared to have him under surveillance. We have reason to believe such surveillance has been used in the past and continues to be used for purposes of blackmail."

Mr. Duncan could not have looked more shocked. "Oh my God. Gentlemen, I promise our full cooperation with your investigation. We do all in our power to maintain the highest levels of excellence in this organization. We are committed to the highest levels of professional service. We want to be the very best at bringing the news to the public. The sort of scandal that could result from what you are suggesting would be devastating. Please let me know anything I can do to be of help in this investigation."

"Thank you Mr. Duncan," Marty spoke forcefully. "We need every file, every receipt, every scrap of paper in this building related to your vans for the last twelve months. We also need a list of every employee who has or has had access to any of these vans. Keep in mind I did not say permission, I said access. We are looking for a criminal with no concern for any rules or regulations."

Mr. Duncan was persuasive in his sincerity. He did not delegate, but called his human resource director, Shelly, to the office with everything about their vans she could get her hands on. The agents got the door for her when only ten minutes later she arrived with a box of files. Mr. Duncan's office was big.

Conferences had taken place there. There was plenty of room to spread out the material and everyone looked over all the material together. Marty started picking pages out of the pile one by one, every one that mentioned Mark. Mark Cason was a mechanic. He had full access to the fleet of vans, and would obviously know them better than anyone. He must have been quite a find for Barbara Hayes.

"I need to know everything you can tell me about Mark Cason." Marty was sharp and serious.

"Is Mark a suspect?" Mr. Duncan asked.

"Everybody listed here is a suspect. Mark looks like the van man. We start at the top."

Shelly related all she knew of Mark Cason. "Mark has been our chief mechanic for six years now. Since he took over we have not had a single van break down. His records are meticulous, mileage logs, gasoline records, all manner of service records, inspections."

Marty countered, "We need copies of all the mileage records. They look good, dates, times, mileage. I see Mark is often out late at night."

Shelly explained, "The vans are mostly in use during the day. So night time is when he can perform road tests. I really think he's the best."

"This does look good," Marty played it cool. "The records can be compared to the mileage needed and the dates surveillance may have taken place. Has there ever been any unusual incidents concerning Mark?"

There was one time over a year ago when Mark had a van out the entire night. He explained that he got a flat tire. He even showed us a picture of the flat tire he had taken. He was very thorough in covering our concerns. But it was unusual."

"Why unusual?"

"We have a number of mechanics on call. The standard procedure is for him to call in and a mechanic would bring him a new tire. It would never take long. And Mark never produced the old tire, which just isn't like him. But it is just one tiny quirk in six years of amazing service. Nothing seems wrong about it."

"Probably nothing," Marty muttered, "But we'll take down the date of that incident."

The agents took down the important notes. Shelly made the copies of the mileage logs. Marty wasn't quite done.

"What can you tell me about Mark personally?"

"Well I must admit with you here asking questions I've been thinking. Like I said no breakdowns in six years. I feel we owe the man. But, thinking about him, he does always seem a bit jumpy. And he really does seem defensive. Everybody thinks he's great, but when you ask him questions he seems to explain way more than necessary. He always has fine answers, we never suspect him. But just the simple questions of routine business he defends himself like he's on trial. He's really great, probably just a bit high strung."

Marty got a look his fellow agents recognized. "I'll have a talk with Mark now."

Agent Robert Dawson, knowing he was on the wire-muttered to himself, "Marty smells blood."

The agents in the van all sat back, looked at each other with dread in their faces, and one of them spoke for the group..."Fasten your seat belts."

Agent Laurie felt her heart beating in her chest. She dismissed it as nerves over this case. She told herself it was very reasonable to be impressed with a professional like Marty. She was certainly the most focused of the bunch.

Shelly led Marty and Robert out into the Bayside News 7 garage area. Mark was under one of the vans. Marty saw the plate had 147 on it. "Perfect," he muttered to himself, but his agents would not miss a word.

"Mark," Shelly called, "Some gentlemen are here to see you."

Mark slid out from under the van and slowly picked himself up to meet his visitors.

Marty spoke first to Shelly, "You can leave now. This is between us and our new friend Mark Cason."

"Okay," Shelly showed great fear and hurried off. That was sure to put Mark in a receptive mood.

"What can I do for you gentlemen?" Mark asked. He did appear to be turning white.

Marty held up his badge and spoke like an Army General. "Federal Bureau of Investigation, my name is Martin Douglas, this is agent Robert Dawson. We need to ask you some questions, and I want you to understand one thing. The FBI does not waste time."

Mark now looked quite like he had seen a ghost. "Okay, I understand. I'm just a mechanic here."

Marty looked at the van. "This is the van. This van was reported seen at the home of John Dreamer Saturday night. I didn't notice any news about Mr. Dreamer on news 7 today. Did you agent Dawson?"

"No sir." Robert played along.

Out in the black van the agents all looked at one another, "Go Marty."

"We can check the wonderful mileage logs, but other evidence from the scene and on this van can confirm our concerns."

Mark weakly spoke up. "I test drive these vans at night. Everything is in my reports."

Marty got in Mark's face like an army general, and his confidence was impenetrable.

"Mr. Cason, do you know why I have not asked to see your identification?"

"No." Mark did not want to speak at all.

"I did not ask to see your identification because I know exactly who you are. You are very photogenic Mr. Cason. Does the name Barbara Hayes mean anything to you?"

"It sounds familiar." Mark was now red and sweating.

"We are investigating Barbara Hayes for blackmail. I believe you know all about this, and your vans and their photography equipment make it all happen. Proving it is another matter. We have plenty of circumstantial evidence on Barbara. But things are looking her way because she is cooperating with authorities. She provided us with a very interesting video tape of you getting out of your black Ford Bronco, getting your tire iron, and loosening the lug nuts on the right rear tire of a Bayside Elementary School bus."

Mark stood there like a ghost, looking like he may need medical attention.

"Let me make something very clear Mr. Mark Cason. School bus security came under direct federal purview when then President George Bush signed H.R. 3162 shortly after the September eleventh attacks in 2001. Part of the administration's broad anti-terrorism initiative is a measure which includes the word "school bus" under the federal definition of a mass transportation system. Under the new law, terrorist acts and other violent crimes against any mass transportation system may be investigated, tried, and punished as a federal crime. You don't begin to know the list of charges you face Mr. Cason, but you will have the rest of your life in prison to sort it out. Miss Hayes has you nailed to the wall."

There was a long moment when it looked as if Mark would explode. Then he did.

"That God dam bitch. Oh God." He paced, he spit, he swung his fists through empty air. Then all Marty could have hoped for and even more came to pass.

"She won't get away with this. No no, she won't get away with this. I've got Barbara Hayes. You've got to help me. I can give you Barbara Hayes, oh believe me, but you've got to help me. This was all Barbara."

Marty softened slightly, looked sideways at Mark and played out this hand.

"Mark, you're facing life. It can't get any worse. I can't make any promises after what you've done. Nobody will want to let this go, innocent children on a school bus. But we do want Barbara. It can only help if you cooperate with us. I can't promise how much, but I personally want Barbara enough to stick my neck out for you. How do you think you can help?"

Mark was not only red, but so angry as to look possessed. "Take me to my house. I've got everything you need there. I just had this thought that she might do something like this. Jesus Christ that bitch. I've got her for you. I always did her dirty work and this is what I get. God," he screamed. "I needed to know if she pulled something like this she would not get away. I've made copies of every letter she sent those people. I've got copies of every check they sent her as down payment. They made them out to cash, but I've made copies of the deposit slips in Barbara's account from those checks. This was all her idea. I just loosened the lug nuts a little bit. I didn't think anybody would get hurt. She gave me $2000.00 for that. And she tapes it?"

Mark let out what could only be described as a growl, followed by every curse word ever invented by man. Marty and Robert looked down at the ground in what was actually an attempt to maintain whatever composure they could. Marty had played the bluff of a lifetime and hit a homerun. But if John dreamed there was a tape of the crime Marty knew there would be. He had played a pretty sure hand.

Out in the black FBI van every agent was speechless. One of them looked at the equipment. "We've got it. This is one for the text books. Pulling a Marty."

Another agent spoke up with no shame. "You have to love this guy. I'll take the first spot in line to shine his shoes."

Agent Laurie looked down at the floor, deep in thought. The words haunted her. "You have to love this guy."

Marty motioned to Robert to put the cuffs on Mr. Cason. "We'll stop by your house on the way to the station. Depending on what you have I may be more help than I thought. I can only promise to do what I can. You have my word on that Mark."

"I have what I said I have. You make sure she knows she didn't take me down without a fight. If I'm going down she is going with me."

Marty thought to himself about his friend John Dreamer. "If this doesn't convince him to work with us nothing will."

23

Lifting Clouds

Leaving the exam room John found Helen waiting with a wheelchair.

"Have a seat John. You know the drill, another trip to the lab, maybe the last trip." Helen teared up. "John, so many times I was afraid it would be the last trip."

John put his hand on Helen's hand and gave her such a smile. "You weren't the only one."

There was silence between them as they walked through the hospital. Helen knew a short cut but it took them through some behind the scenes areas. She wheeled her patient carefully with both of them intent on minding their own business and respecting the privacy of others, but a scream from a patient room caused them both to look in. They looked just as a blanket was being pulled over a man who looked to be John's age. An older woman, perhaps his mother, wept with all of her being. No words needed to be shared between John and Helen. The sound of the wheels on the floor was strangely comforting, but John's thoughts remained on his resemblance to the man he had just seen. He vowed not to lose his grip on how precious it was to be alive. He put his hand on Helen's once again. She gave it a squeeze.

When they reached the lab a very pretty nurse spoke up, "I'll take him from here Helen. We'll call you when he's ready to go back."

"My name is Terry. I'll be taking you to your room. We have a room set up because the doctor wants a bone marrow test along with the blood work."

John closed his eyes, but he did mutter "Thank you." The bone marrow tests hurt. John got to thinking of how much pain he had endured over the years. Just as Helen hoped her suffering made her a better nurse, John hoped he was a better man for having known the worst of life. A man he had just passed a moment ago could no longer feel anything. John was still in the game. He was placed on a gurney and Terry wheeled him down a long hallway. Suddenly they struck somebody.

Dr. Tom Brady had blocked their path on purpose. "John Dreamer, we meet again."

Dr. Brady looked impressive enough when he wasn't towering over a gurney. This sight was imposing indeed. John felt like a child brought to the principal's office.

"Oh yes, Hi Dr. Brady. I remember." John smiled.

"Well Mr. Dreamer, you are looking very well indeed. Would you care to explain how that is possible?"

John sat up partway on his elbows, looked Dr. Brady in the eyes, and said, "Great coffee."

Dr. Brady didn't flinch. He turned to Terry. "I'll take Mr. Dreamer to his room. I want to see that these tests are carried out properly."

"Okay thanks. Let me know when you want him brought back to Dr. Bernard's office."

"I may handle that as well."

John was set in his room, told it may be a while, and offered a magazine or TV.

"No thanks, I'll rest for a bit."

From his bed he could see Dr. Brady reading his chart, and looking at the computer screen. John closed his eyes. He did want to rest, but it became more of a meditation. He had just seen the loss of life, a loss he had faced so many times. He remembered coming out of the water after taking Fusheeswa. He saw Kari's precious face smiling at him. He knew, he just knew she was somewhere in a hospital too. She was comforting patients, running tests. He wondered what her specialty could be. He bet she was great with pediatrics. John forgot all about everything except Kari. Missing her became like a physical hunger. The hospital environment was hers and she should be here. And somehow he was hers, and they should be together. But then other thoughts clouded his mind. A gorgeous nurse like that, all the doctors should be all over her. How could she be single or available? It was as if his thoughts tried to talk him out of dreaming. But he could see her beautiful face, and a diamond tear, "Find me John, I need you more than anything."

She needed him. His mind still fought him. Did she need him just to bring her to Helen? But then he heard again what he needed to hear. He heard Kari's voice as if he was dreaming again, "My John." And she had called herself, "Your Kari," when he spoke her name. She had said Heaven was the time they spent together. Lying there in the hospital John realized his primary diagnoses was "Hopelessly in love." It was a progressive condition for which there was no cure. He would use all his strength to work out the Richard's case, but Kari had to be everything after that. Whatever finding her could mean, or however he could make it happen, the rest of his life was dedicated to her.

"Sorry to have kept you waiting, we're busy today." John didn't even bother to look at this man's name tag. He did get a glimpse of the needle. He always wished he wouldn't see the darn needle. He wanted to believe they had come up with a smaller version since his last visit, but no such luck.

"Roll on your side. I'll try to make this as quick and painless as possible."

"Oh thank you very much." John's heart was not in that

comment. He knew it. And as he could not let go of his thoughts of Kari he willed his thoughts to her. "My heart is with you."

There really is nothing like physical pain to bring focus and clarity back in the worst way. John was quickly aware he was just a patient in Bayside Medical Center, relieved as hell when it was over and a bandage was placed on the needle mark. Nurses slowly laid him back down. He felt like he had been shot and was being laid to rest.

It was probably another half hour that he lay there just feeling all his love for Kari. It was like a weight on his chest. He wanted to be crushed by her, to feel her weight pressing on him bringing them together as close as possible.

Finally, there was a shadow cast across the whole room. Once again, a very imposing Dr. Tom Brady stood over him. His demeanor was very serious. John thought it so unfair that anyone in this place could be angry with him. All he had ever done was try to live. And it had always seemed so unnecessarily difficult.

Dr. Brady spoke. "Mr. John Dreamer, you have been with us for the past five years living under the dark cloud of a cancer diagnoses, and finally Leukemia. As you know I am chief of staff at this hospital. I am ultimately responsible for what goes on here, the lives saved by every hero who works here, and the lives lost because some conditions still beat science to the finish line. Nothing makes me happier than to bring good news. Mr. Dreamer, I'll spare you details about hematopoietic cells and fat cells, but we now find no evidence of any illness or condition in your body what so ever."

John sighed and tears streamed from his eyes. This weight taken from him, this dark cloud finally lifted, Kari had somehow done this for him. But what was the greater miracle was that the impossible thanks that he owed her was possible, if he could find her and take her to Helen. He was dazed in his thoughts but looked at Dr. Brady.

Dr. Brady continued. "John, in spite of this most astonishing news I am not happy. I am not happy because we have no explanation for this cure. Your case has left us with a greater question than it brought to us in the first place. I am asking you John, how did this happen? All our patients drink coffee. This is life and death Mr. Dreamer, and I want to share good news with more cancer patients. So I have to ask you how do you account for what has happened here?"

John stared into space for a moment, but then he looked Dr. Brady in the eye. Tears streamed down his face once again. He didn't try to stop them.

"Dr. Brady, there is someone I would like you to meet some day. She is a nurse outside this hospital who I met this year. She gave me something. It may not have been something that could cure everybody, but Dr. Brady," John spoke very slowly; "I felt it curing me."

Dr. Brady's face seemed less pained, but even more intense.

"What did she give you?"

John sat up, put his hand on Dr. Brady's hand, and looked him in the eye again through his tears. "A reason to live."

There was a decent moment of silence. Dr. Brady's face softened. He got a sly grin and raised his eyebrows.

"Well why didn't you just say so?" Now he openly smiled and shook his head. "Does Helen know?"

"Helen knows everything," John spoke with strength returning to his voice.

"Well let's go tell her about these test results. I'm sure she can't wait to hear about hematopoietic cells and fat cells."

John gave a thumb's up.

24

Afternoon Escape

Steven Richards struck the steering wheel in his car a few times. He hated being stuck in traffic, but he had left enough time so that he probably wouldn't be late for his next appointment. He had shown two houses that morning and had hopes of showing at least two more this afternoon. The morning had been promising. And above all, he was away from the office. For whatever reason, Barbara had become a terror from hell as the day wore on. Steven didn't know why she was so agreeable to let him handle showing the houses today, but he jumped at the chance. He didn't think he was half bad either in spite of lack of practice. Barbara almost always handled the customers. They all asked about her. They actually spoke so highly of her. It made Steven ill.

"If only they knew?" He spoke out loud. Traffic picked up again and he would be fine. Susan had a dental appointment tomorrow morning so he had to wind up this day and get home earlier than usual. Thoughts of home filled him with such guilt. He did not deserve his family. Nothing was more certain to him. He thought of his beautiful Susan almost every moment. How could he ever have betrayed her? He did not love Barbara. He was paralyzed to the point of stupid where Barbara was concerned. Nothing he ever did was good enough for her. He would not sleep with her again, but he had taken advantage of her one night. He couldn't deny that, and she had the proof. For Steven it was like a mathematical problem he wrestled with every single day. He looked at the mess he made of his life and couldn't figure it out. What pieces could he move where? Why wouldn't Barbara leave him alone?

Thoughts of John Dreamer haunted him. John seemed so nice and decent, but what did he want? Steven was afraid maybe Susan had hired a private investigator. He remembered John's words, "Is Barbara your nightmare?" What did John know? Life had become a nightmare for Steven. "What did I do to deserve this?" He spoke up again.

Then he heard John's voice just as it had been that night at dinner. "I'll show you some day." Steven slammed on the brakes just in time. He was stopped at another light. He had to get a grip. There had not been any more word from John. It must be just his nerves. He was close to arriving at the apartment of his next client. His thoughts returned to Susan. He thought about sleeping next to her each night. He had been the luckiest man in the world. How could he have been so stupid? The only consolation he clung to was the feeling that he was paying for his failure. Each day a living hell was just what he deserved.

"Shit," Barbara yelled as she slammed down the phone again. She had been trying all day to contact Mark Cason. He didn't answer his cell phone. His work said he was, "Not available." "Not available. What the F...is not available? Is he there or not? He better F...'n get available." With Steven away she had the pictures of John and Susan laid out in front of her. "What a lovely couple." If looks could kill that couple would be dead. Barbara wanted to get a package to Susan soon, and she wanted Mark to deliver it as always. "Where the hell is he?" Barbara had no way of knowing she was finished before she even started. Mark was checking out their new home.

Barbara lay out the pictures across the conference room table. There were several photos of Susan in her car, then John driving up. A close up photo showed Susan crying. A series of shots showed John taking Susan by the hand. She slowly got out of the car and rose to him. Good shots of the hand holding. Then there were several photos of John and Susan holding each other tightly. Barbara got excited. "Guess I shouldn't be so mad at Mark after all. Not a bad night's work. What else do we have?"

Barbara slipped other photos out of the envelope. She looked at Susan and John holding hands across the table from one another.

"Whatcha got there?" Barbara let out a scream and almost jumped out of her skin. She turned to see Marty and Robert standing beside her.

"Why that looks like pictures of John Dreamer and Susan Richards. Now how could you possibly have those?"

It was Barbara's turn to be a ghost. "Who are you? You're trespassing, get out of this office."

Marty smiled. He held up his FBI badge. "Hi Barbara. I've been looking forward to meeting you. I'm agent Martin Douglas, this is agent Robert Dawson. We're here to arrest you for blackmail, conspiracy to commit acts of terrorism, conspiracy to commit murder. This warrant says I can collect those pictures now. This is one package you won't be sending. Thanks to Mark Cason we have copies of everything you have sent, and copies of checks made out to cash by your victims, and...copies of deposit slips from the deposit of those checks into your bank account, nobody else's."

"Why?" Barbara screamed at the top of her lungs. She kept screaming, "Why? Why? Why?"

Marty looked at her with disgust, then he motioned to Robert. "Read her her rights and cuff her."

"Wait," Barbara screamed out. "Mark is the criminal here. He tried to make a school bus full of children crash. I've got it all on video tape. I'm not the bad one here."

Marty turned away for just a second to take a breath and get a grasp on his composure. Then he spoke up. "It will certainly be in your best interest to cooperate here Ms. Hayes. We're going to have to take you in to the station, but we can pick up that video tape and let you collect some belongings."

Barbara wept. "It wasn't supposed to turn out this way. I'm not the cheating spouse. I never betrayed anybody. Those people deserved what they got. I don't deserve this. Everyone I've ever loved has betrayed me."

Marty shook his head. "You are going to have a lot of time to clear your head. Maybe you will learn to see things differently."

Robert led Barbara outside while Marty collected the evidence from Barbara's office. Before leaving the building, Marty took an extra look around Richard's Realty. "This place could use some family pictures."

25

Moving Right Along

Helen looked up from one of her patient charts to see none other than Dr. Tom Brady pushing John in his wheelchair. "I've got something for you Helen, the healthiest specimen in Bayside."

He had not meant to embarrass Helen, but she could not hold it together after those words. She covered her face, but plenty of tears escaped. John got up out of his wheelchair and gave her the hug of a lifetime.

"Don't forget Mr. Dreamer, I will want to meet that other nurse you told me about."

When she was able to pull herself together enough Helen asked John what he had told Dr. Brady about Kari.

With that far away look he so often possessed John let the words slip out of his mouth, "The truth."

"How are you feeling John?" Helen got back to business.

"Like I've had enough needles for a lifetime, pretty sore."

"I did have one or two in mind for later. Dr. Bernard is fine with my staying late and using the rooms. We should get a little something to eat. Then maybe you can rest. I have chart reviews to do that can keep me busy into the night."

"A bite would be fine." John was hungry.

Steven thought his business had gone well for today. He was

surprised he had not heard from Barbara, and she did not answer at the office. But he was very thankful for the good fortune. Susan would have a great meal waiting for him. She was so excited he would actually be home that night. Thinking about it brought on the guilt again. Once again, the mathematics puzzle got his mind spinning. He questioned his involvement with Barbara. One night of too much to drink and he was a ruined man. It didn't make any sense to him. Something was missing and he couldn't figure it out. He had no idea what would happen if he would sleep on it.

After a light dinner, John and Helen went back to the offices of Dr. Bernard. Helen worked on her chart reviews and John did look over some magazines. His back hurt and he was fine with resting.

Back at the Bayside FBI field office the group of agents who had been working the Richard's case met in the conference room. David sat at the head of the table with the evidence now in a power point presentation. He projected everything on a screen on the wall.

"Five blackmail letters, all similar. We're matching it to Barbara's equipment but there is no doubting any of this. Agent Douglas this has got to be your finest hour."

Marty had to eat it up some, but he had another agenda.

"I need to call your attention to a very important detail in every single one of these letters. They are all very specific on one point, all of them. That is Steven Richards is not to be told about any of the transactions or the incriminating photos will be published immediately. None of the victims we have interviewed thus far gave any indication that Steven Richards had any knowledge of these transactions or had any part in the black mail schemes." Marty got quiet for a moment, somewhat emotional. Laurie couldn't keep her eyes off of him for a minute.

He spoke up again. "This has been one incredible day. None of this could have happened without John Dreamer. I acted on his information because I believe in him totally. I don't know if

I can ever get him to help us again, but I'll be hounding him the rest of his life about it."

David added his take on it. "Marty, you just have to be careful about these things. The man impressed me. I'll give you that."

"I know to be careful." Marty started to look at Laurie. He was a legend at finding the clues for his cases, but perhaps he had missed what was most important for his own life.

"I've always believed John Dreamer. But I have to admit, I want to believe him. I need him to be correct."

Laurie wondered why Marty had been looking at her. It was almost as if he had been talking to her alone. She smiled to herself because she had a secret. She couldn't stop thinking about how amazing Marty was. An eight-month investigation and he nailed it shut in a couple of hours.

David went over more specifics of the case. Those two "wing nuts" had certainly convicted each other. Marty had caught Barbara in the act with the pictures of John and Susan. It could spare them any embarrassment. It would most likely be possible to protect all the individuals involved. Confessions are as good as it gets and Barbara and Mark had fallen completely for the "Tricks of the trade." The physical evidence was absolutely conclusive.

When the meeting was over Marty got a few high fives. Some of the agents wanted to go out for dinner. Marty declined and started to pack up some of his things. Laurie was also busy with packing up her things, laptop, briefcase, and purse. When it became just the two of them in the room she shook her head and did speak to Marty.

"You sure are amazing. You were so fearless going out on a limb like that. Is there anything you're not good at?"

Marty looked at Laurie, and he seemed strangely shy. "I have no problem with criminals, knife fights, being shot at. But do you think I can ask a girl out on a date?"

As the two of them looked at each other smiles evolved on their faces.

Then Laurie took Marty by surprise. "Did John tell you about me?"

Marty had no cool about him now. He looked like a kid with his hand caught in the cookie jar.

"Well he might have mentioned something."

"I told him to," Laurie winked. Then she pointed a finger at him like a gun, "Bingo."

26

Dream Repair

It had been an emotional day to say the least. "Are you getting sleepy?" Helen asked him through a pretty big yawn.

"I think I've had enough for one day. I just hope I have the energy for working through my sleep."

"Well wash up and get in one of our lovely designer gowns for the evening Mr. Dreamer, your room is ready."

"Yes mother. Will you read me a story?"

Steven crawled into bed next to Susan. She spoke softly to him. "It has been so nice to have you home on a Monday night." She leaned over and kissed him.

"Thank you. And thanks so much for that wonderful dinner. You're a great cook."

"Is that why you married me?"

Steven was silent for perhaps too long. "You're a great everything. I just got too lucky?"

"You can be lucky." Susan remembered the good times.

Steven couldn't escape his mode of going through the motions. "I sure hope everything goes well with your dental appointment in the morning. I hate those things."

With the lights out Steven couldn't see the tears on Susan's face. He had managed to escape the pain he caused very well. It was time for his real nightmare.

"Good night," Susan whispered. She did sniffle. Maybe Steven heard that.

Back in a hospital bed Helen tucked John in very tightly. She fastened him in with restraints. She put the oxygen monitor on one of his fingers, put on a blood pressure cuff, hooked him up to telemetry, and started an IV. There were ports along the IV tube. "I know you only wanted one needle."

"I didn't want any."

"Well tough it up boy, I know what I'm doing...I think." Helen put a nasal cannula in his nose to give him more oxygen. She took his free hand in hers. "John, good luck. I'll be right here. You have a good sleep, as good as possible. You're a good man. I'll be watching you like a hawk. Anything goes wrong I'm on it."

John spoke up. "You might as well get comfortable yourself. This could be a long night. Take it easy. I can holler if I need you."

"I hope so." Helen whispered. "Good night for now."

John closed his eyes. He could feel the oxygen going into his nose, but it was comfortable. The tightly tucked sheets gave him warmth that was soothing. He breathed deeply to relax. He focused his attention on Steven Richards. He remembered each picture he had seen of Steven in better times. He remembered their meetings, sitting at the table pondering Barbara, the hand shakes. He remembered Steven's office. He felt himself there in that office looking around, just standing there in Richard's Realty.

Then it became lighter. Steven appeared next to him. The two of them stood in Richard's Realty. It looked different. It looked way friendlier. There were pictures of Steven's family all over the place.

"What is this?" Steven asked, obviously frightened.

John looked at Steven and took charge. This was his domain. "Steven Richards, this is a day we better look at...together."

141

"What is this?" Steven cried?

"Look and see Steven." John was firm. "We're dreaming together, you and me. But this is more than just a dream. Watch."

As the two of them stood there in that dream world Steven could see Barbara at her desk. Then they saw Steven come in. He looked so much better then. He called to his assistant, "Good morning Barbara." Barbara waved.

John and Steven watched the Steven of last year head into his office. He sat down and turned on his computer. The desk top was a beautiful picture of Susan. They could see Steven's face beaming. The phone rang. Steven grabbed it.

"Hi Honey," it was Susan's beautiful voice. "You know I miss you already. I hope you don't get tired of hearing from me."

Steven beamed, "Never."

"Well I want to thank you for last night, again. For reading to the kids, and then showing me your not so little engine that could."

The dreaming Steven turned to John, "You shouldn't be hearing this. We shouldn't be here."

John turned to Steven, "I shouldn't be hearing this?"

Suddenly they were in Barbara's office. They could see Barbara was listening in on her extension to everything Steven and Susan said. They could hear the lovers over the phone, and saw Barbara push the button to hang up when it was over. Barbara muttered to herself, "The little engine that could. Well we'll see if we can't derail this train."

"What is going on?" Steven cried out.

"That is what we're here to find out," John replied.

Suddenly they were in Barbara's apartment. It was evening of that same day. Barbara was charming Steven with ideas for publicity concerning their business. She spoke with such enthusiasm, "Steven thanks for coming over. This will just take a little while. I want to show you what I've been working on. Get comfortable. I'll get us a drink, I've been working hard on some ideas and I just really want to share them with you."

"Okay, I appreciate that." Steven seemed innocent enough.

But John and Steven in that dream world could follow Barbara and see what she was doing. She poured the drinks, but then she put some substance in Steven's drink.

"What is that?" Steven cried out to John.

"I believe it is called Rohypnol."

John and Steven watched as Barbara and Steven looked over photos Barbara had taken and sheets she had typed. But they could see Steven was fading fast. Barbara made mention of it. "Hey, drinking a little fast there?" She put her arm on his shoulder and started to rub it gently. "Does that feel good?"

"Yes it feels very good thank you," Steven spoke kindly, but he was slurring. "I'm sorry I seem to be a little sleepy."

Barbara walked around behind the sofa where they had been seated and started to rub the back of his neck. "You've been under a lot of stress. A man should feel good in the evening after a hard day's work. I think you should lie down for a little while. Its Okay, I have a comfortable bed. I'm sure you'll like it."

Barbara loosened a couple of buttons on her blouse and put some cleavage in Steven's face. Steven was on the verge of passing out. It was a pleasant sight to pass into. "Oh that's nice," Steven slurred and then slumped over.

It was all Barbara could do to get Steven up and drag him into her bedroom. Once she had him in the bed she undressed him and hooked up a lot of camera equipment, pointing it right at the bed. Then she got undressed herself and climbed in.

"Oh My God," the dreaming Steven was literally beside himself.

"Oh my God. I can't believe this. All this time I thought I took advantage of her. Jesus Christ. She did this. For all the blame she put on me she did this. This was all her doing. I'm the victim here!"

143

"Not so fast Steven," John was dead serious, "This isn't over."

They watched as Steven woke up and found himself in bed with Barbara. Barbara acted very satisfied. She spoke up in a seductive voice, "Well baby, thanks for showing me a not so little engine that really could."

John and Steven watched as Steven regained some senses, but not enough.

"What happened?" He asked Barbara.

"You better remember what happened. You gave me the night of my life. I love you too. And this is all on tape so I can relive every precious moment until we can be together permanently."

Steven was hurt, confused, pathetic, but he was trying to piece it all together. He reluctantly had to believe what it looked like. And how else could Barbara know about the engine that could?

Now John and Steven both knew the truth. The mathematics puzzle could finally be laid to rest. Steven was in shock, but he also felt the burden of a lifetime lift from his being.

"God, all this time I thought I had hurt her, but she hurt me. I'm the victim here. All this time I was completely innocent."

Suddenly they were in a dark room. It was like a police interrogation room. Steven was sitting, John standing over him, and John was angry.

"What is it?" Steven asked.

"Steven Richards, what I'm about to show you will make or break you. Do you understand me?"

"I don't know what this is all about. What can you show me?"

"You are not worthy of the title "Victim" but I am going to show you who is."

"What?" Steven gasped.

Suddenly John held up an old instamatic camera. "Susan makes very beautiful photo albums. I've never met anyone who loves her family as much as she does. She treasures everything.

And she makes the albums for her family to treasure. We are going to see the Steven Richard's photo album."

"What do you mean?" Steven got very distressed.

"Where are we?" He asked.

They were in the hair and nail salon. John and Steven together watching the events unfold. Peggy approached Susan. "Susan Richards I can't believe it. God how long has it been? Why do we let so much time slip away?"

The words of Steven's beautiful wife, "Gosh I don't know. I just know it is so good to see you. Thank God you were here today of all days."

"Well its Saturday Honey- that will do it. Come here on a Saturday and you've found me."

Susan bursts into tears. Peggy is shocked and asks, "Are you Okay?"

Through her heart breaking tears Susan cries, "I'm sorry, I just don't get out much and I guess I'm not good at it."

Flash! John took the picture of Susan's misery. "Here's picture number one for your album." John spoke with disgust in his voice. "Here is Susan Richards with her husband all out of sorts for no good reason."

"Oh my God," Steven cried. "Oh Susan. Oh my God, what have I done?"

Then, in an instant, they were in Steven and Susan's bedroom. Susan was on the phone late at night. She was listening to it ring over and over. She cried out over and over, "Where is he? Where is he?" She slammed her purse down on the bed.

Flash! "Photo number two. You think you were the victim? We're just getting started." John was pulling no punches.

Tears started to stream down Steven's face.

Next they could see Susan meeting with John. They could hear every word she said. "I've just loved Steven so much always, right from the beginning." She cries as she pleads with John, "I need you to be for real."

Flash. "Photo number three. Your wife as desperate as can be. She is the victim here."

"No," Steven cried out. "Stop."

"You didn't stop it Steven. Any moment you could have said enough is enough. You could have claimed your love. But all you wanted was to save your pride. We're not done."

Standing outside the hospital Susan comes running up to John. "Danny's bus was in an accident, he's been taken here." Susan looked so pained.

John speaks, "We'll find him. I'm sure he's alright. Will we meet Steven?"

"Steven said to keep him posted." Susan wipes away a tear. Flash! "We've got plenty of pages to fill in your photo album Steven." John looked intently at Steven Richards.

"John, I am so sorry. I don't know what was the matter with me. I can't believe it."

They next see John and Danny in the emergency room. John looks full of love as he speaks. "That must have been quite an accident. You'll have quite a story to tell Dad."

"By the time I see Dad I'll forget it."

Flash! "And your children, Danny and Caitlin. Do you have any idea what a blessed man you have been Steven? These are the innocent victims. Innocent. This is who paid the price for your mess."

"Oh my God," was all Steven could say.

Suddenly they found themselves at the door to the Richard's home. "Your family is in there. Can you go home?" John blurted out.

"I want to go home," Steven cried out. But as he entered the home he seemed to crash through the floor as if it was ice.

Steven landed in what felt like warm water beneath the floor level. He treaded water beneath the floor. The floor was like dirty ice. He couldn't get out. He was drifting more into the house away from the hole where he had fallen in. He could make out John walking on the floor above him.

"John help me," Steven yelled.

"I am helping you, believe it or not." He held up the camera. "Just a few more shots to finish your album Steven."

"No please, no." Steven treaded the water. He looked around, but he was helpless.

"Your family can't hear you, just as you didn't hear them. You need to hear them."

Steven drifted under Caitlin's room. Caitlin sat there on the bed next to John. She spoke to John. "Can you be my new Daddy? I want a daddy that reads to me."

Steven heard the kind words John spoke about how lucky he was, and that perhaps he just needed to be reminded how important it was to read to his daughter.

"John help me. I'm so sorry. I swear. I have no excuse, I was just so afraid."

Flash! The camera spit out another picture. Caitlin crying. John put it in the album.

"This is your family for the last year. Here's another one."

"No," Steven cried and chocked as he worked to keep his head above the water.

They were now at Danny's birthday party, but Danny was crying his eyes out. "Where's Daddy? He promised Mommy. He promised he would be here."

Flash! The camera spit out another photo of the suffering of the Richards family.

John got down on his hands and knees. He put this last picture in the album. Steven splashed about but couldn't do anything about his circumstances.

John spoke to him. "So Steven, what do you have to say? What is your plan? What are you going to do?"

Steven screamed, "John."

Susan jumped out of bed. Steven was dreaming. It had to be

just as John Dreamer had said. Whatever he could do, he was doing it. Steven had screamed John's name. He was thrashing about in the bed. Susan was terrified, but she didn't dare touch him.

Steven slipped under the water for a moment, but came back up. "John, anything to get them back. Oh God John, anything to get them back."

Tears streamed out of Susan's eyes as she heard Steven crying. Could he be talking about her and their family? Did he want them back? She wept in prayer that this is what was happening.

"Steven look at me," John called to him through that strange dirty ice. "Do you see this?" He held up the photo album.

"Yes," Steven gasped.

"Do you see this?" John held up a cigarette lighter.

"Yes," Steven gasped again.

"Your family Steven. Your family deserves a second chance. They want you back. You are all they've ever wanted Steven Richards. They deserve your love. All of it Steven. Every bit of love you have"

"I love my family John, I love my family." Steven cried so deeply.

Susan wept as she heard every word.

John put the lighter to that dreaded photo album and it quickly burned to ashes which he blew away.

"Then it is time Steven. Time to go home."

John raised his fists and slammed through that dark ice and raised Steven up.

Steven found him self sitting in his bed. Susan wept on her knees beside the bed. He was weeping just as hard. "Oh my God Susan. I am so sorry. I am so sorry, oh my God."

There was knocking on their bedroom door as the kids had heard crying. Susan looked to Steven. He begged her, "Let them in."

It was the most incredible moment of tears and love Susan had ever known. She tired to believe in what was happening. It was too good to be true.

"Are you Okay?" Danny and Caitlin were so worried about Daddy.

Steven pleaded with his family. "Danny, Caitlin, Susan, I have not been Okay. I am so sorry." He could hardly talk he was crying so hard, but he was also smiling.

Danny asked him a question. "Did John help you? He's our friend and I know he wanted to help you."

Steven started to laugh through his tears. "Yes Danny. John came and helped me. He showed me just what I needed to see. He helped me get back on the track. Just like the little engine that could." The family held each other tight as could be.

Helen had seen John seem somewhat agitated, now he got very still. She looked up at the monitors. Blood pressure was dropping, heart rate was dropping.

"I hate this part," she muttered.

"Okay John, I think that's enough. It's time for you to wake up."

John was drifting toward a fountain in the middle of a city. It was a beautiful setting, but rather dark at night. Ornate street lights like candles made it breath taking. He could see Kari sitting beside the fountain. He could never grasp how beautiful she was. You really can't remember it; you have to look at her. "Kari," he called out. But she couldn't hear him. This was different. He could see her, but it was like he wasn't there. He sat beside her. "Kari it's me." There was no response.

Helen started tapping John on the shoulder. "John wake up, enough already."

John sat back in silence. Nothing mattered but to look at her. She was enjoying the beauty of this new special place. Kari had some kind of sketch pad and appeared to be drawing a picture of this enchanting scene. A beautiful fountain with the water drops lit up by the lights like thousands of diamonds falling from above.

"You've done it again. Found a place beautiful enough for you to fit in," John whispered in her ear. Then he looked deep in her eyes because he could get close this time. "I love you."

Kari suddenly smiled. She looked around smiling. She couldn't see anything, but she felt happiness. She somehow knew he was there. She put down the pad.

"John, are you finding me?" She kept looking all around but couldn't see him.

The tears and smile blended on his face. He took a quick glance around. This was some beautiful city. There was a sign but it was too far off in the distance and it was too dark. He thought he could make out a big letter "D."

"Kari," he spoke. "I love you with all my heart. I will do whatever it takes to find you, I promise."

Kari kept looking around like she knew he had to be right there. For some reason she just wasn't allowed to see him this time.

"I love you John." Hearing those words was enough to stop his heart. That is what they did.

"Oh Jesus," Helen yelled. She cleared everything off of John and got the automated external defibrillator on him in a flash. It took seconds to charge.

Helen yelled, "Come back to me John. Come back to me. Come back to me."

Much could be written about magic words. But truth isn't just stranger than fiction. It is stronger. Those words "Come back to me." They passed through an eternal void and flew where only love could take them.

"Come back to me." Kari jumped. Her sketch pad fell to the pavement, her pencils scattered. She looked in all directions, almost at once. She sat back down huddled in a fetal position beside the fountain. Then she looked again- everywhere, but there was nothing she could see. But she had heard something, heard it with her heart and not her ears.

"Come back to me."

Kari cried out the plea she had always hidden in her heart. "Mom?"

The defibrillator shocked John. He shook briefly. He took stock of his surroundings as if he had just been dropped into this new world.

Helen studied all the telemetry readings which had lit up the screen again. She let out a cosmic sigh of relief. She was ecstatic, but also disgusted. She let John have it. "Man you just made me age another year. Scare a poor old woman half to death. What have you got to say for yourself?"

John looked like he had been through a war zone, but he knew just what he had to say. "How many cities begin with the letter D?"

Helen laughed and shook her head. "Too many."

27

Wake Up Call

It was three o'clock in the afternoon Tuesday when the phone rang in John's apartment. He had been up once before to use the bathroom but didn't even know what time that was. He was not tucked in tightly this time. Without any thought, he picked up the receiver and greeted Helen. "Hi Helen."

Helen tightened her lips and looked at the phone before she spoke. "John do you have caller ID?"

"No," he spoke, and started to realize what had happened.

"Well you can't just Hi Helen me and everybody else who calls. You will get yourself in trouble."

John sat up and pondered how he felt. "Helen I can't believe it is three o'clock in the afternoon. I must have been thoroughly exhausted. I knew it was you calling. I can't explain that. Ever since that Fusheeswa I have felt so alive."

Helen answered but her voice broke, "Well last night you were so dead."

John could hear Helen crying. After the dream work she had kept him in that hospital bed for observation most of the night. She finally drove him home just before she had to get back to work. She was the one who should be exhausted. He told her that.

She replied, "Well I can miss a night's sleep once in a while, but my butt is certainly dragging today. That's part of why I'm calling. I sure needed to check up on you, but I also don't feel like cooking tonight. Is it alright if I stop by your place tonight with Chinese?"

"Are you kidding? My favorite nurse and a big bag of Chinese food, I'm in Heaven." He almost said he had died and gone to Heaven, but he understood how difficult the night had been for Helen. Nothing was funny about it. He also knew the real reason she wanted to come over, but he kept quiet about it.

"Well I figure I'll be getting there around five thirty. Is that alright?"

"Perfect Helen, thank you so much. Helen…I thank God for you every day."

"Likewise John. I'm glad you slept. How are you feeling?"

"Rested thank you and I've suddenly got this craving for Chinese food."

"That's my John." Helen felt better, but still worried. She really needed the chance to visit with John and talk. "See you soon."

John sat up and stretched. He was feeling very good. He was rested. It had been quite a night. He wondered how things were going with the Richards family. He wouldn't call. They would certainly contact him soon enough. He fed Sebastian and gave him fresh water.

"Sorry I was so sleepy there fellow." He smiled as he watched the big cat dig in, and visions of Chinese food danced in his head.

The phone rang again. He immediately knew it was Marty, but he remembered what Helen had said.

"Hello," he spoke into the phone. He felt funny, but it was also strange how much he seemed to know.

"Hey John, it's Marty. How are you buddy?"

"Well it was a rough night of dreaming. You know I do that under medical supervision, and this was a tough one. So what's with you and Laurie?" John had crossed a line he had better learn not to cross like that. There was a long moment of silence as he realized what he had said.

"John you're scaring me," Marty was not even half joking. "We had our first date last night and I can't get her out of my mind, or apparently, yours."

John took a deep breath. He knew about their date. He knew what restaurant they went to, what food they ordered, what dress Laurie was wearing. He had become accustomed to some heightened level of sensitivity, and had stopped questioning his sanity over what he could do with his dreams. But this was something else happening to him. He had to get a grip on it fast.

"I'm sorry if I scared you. I just had a good feeling about you two. Looks like I was on to something."

"Well I didn't expect it but I somehow managed to ask her out. I think I probably did alright but this scared me. I honestly can't remember a better night in my life."

"Sounds like you're in trouble." John was getting his grip.

"Speaking of trouble, the reason I'm calling is to tell you your trouble with the Richard's case is over. I don't want to discuss this over the phone, but I didn't want you stressing. Believe me when I tell you it is over. Barbara Hayes and Mark Cason are done, Steven is in the clear. No more over the phone. I want to take you to dinner tomorrow. I have a special place in mind. We can talk and get caught up."

John was very relieved to hear that news. He wondered how things could possibly be wrapped up in that amount of time. He spoke up about it. "Isn't there a meeting tomorrow night with David and your team with the Richards family?"

"John I was at a meeting with Steven and Susan today, very nice couple. I had to explain to Steven that he had lost an employee, and of course fill him in. He didn't seem to mind a bit about losing Barbara. He's very upset about what she did with his clients. Barbara will be paying a heavy price for that, but enough over the phone."

"How did Steven and Susan seem to you?" John was on edge.

"Well I noticed they never let go of each other, held hands the whole time."

John sensed that Marty and Laurie had shared a brief goodnight kiss last night, and both of them were in awe over each other. He kept his grip.

"So you want to take me to dinner? Do I get picked up in an awesome Town car?"

"You sure do. John, what I owe you...I just will never find the words."

"What are you talking about?" John smiled.

"John the way I wrapped up the Richards case, I looked and felt like some kind of super hero. And this happens in front of Laurie. I was on such a cloud I didn't even know what I was doing and I ask her out. Oh my God. None of this..." Marty got quiet for a moment. "John none of this would have happened without your help."

"Yeah, I'd say you owe me dinner." John laughed.

"I've got to go John. Be ready at six thirty. Wear a tie."

"So this isn't Burger King?"

"Not exactly. See you tomorrow. Goodnight."

"Goodnight Marty. Thanks for calling."

John took his time putting the phone down. He put his hand over his face and tried to focus. He had a mental storm to deal with now. His powers of perception had grown nearly beyond his ability to handle them. That, along with the fact that the dream had nearly killed him just filled his brain with questions. It would be very good to talk with Helen. She always seemed to come along and save him. He hoped she could do it yet again.

The time passed very quickly and he heard Helen at the door. It was always a blessed reunion now.

"Special delivery for the Dreamer residence," Helen was very relieved to see John looking good.

"You are just the best. How did I get so lucky?"

"Darned if I know. I do have a little business I want to take care of first though. Off with your shirt and sit yourself down."

John knew what was in her big pocket book. Blood pressure cuff and stethoscope. He obliged. Helen was as thorough as Dr. Bernard. She listened to his heart exactly as he did, putting the stethoscope in the same places, having him breathe deeply. She shined a light in his eyes. She had him sit with one leg over the other and checked his reflexes. Then she took his blood pressure. "Okay, still a teenager. Very good John."

"I don't know if I wish that or not. I'm sure in love like one, and I'm not the only one."

"What do you mean?' Helen was very curious at that.

"My friend Marty who works for the FBI. I gave him a little push in the right direction and it seems to be working out well."

Helen dished up the food, and when they were ready she said grace. Then she looked over at John with sadness in her eyes. "We do need to talk John."

"I know. There is plenty to talk about. You can go first." John passed the buck.

"John we've been working together for a few years now in this amazing dream business. I filled you in a little more this past time about what I'm doing while you are dreaming. I do watch you like a hawk. It has been difficult before near the end of your dreams, but last night…" Tears streamed down Helen's face. "John just a few hours after getting the best news I could ever pray for about your health…" It was very difficult to talk. "Just a few hours later I watched all your vital signs drop, and then you flat lined John. You flat lined. I thought I would die. I would have wished it was me."

"I'm so sorry Helen," John shook his head.

"John I don't think we should do this anymore."

There was a very long silence. Neither one of them really had to speak. It was like a long moment of silence given for deep reflection over tremendous loss.

John finally broke the silence. "Helen, I want to live. I want to live more than I ever thought possible. There have been plenty of times I sure wanted to bag all my suffering. This miracle of a second chance, or who knows how many chances it has been, but Fusheeswa…" The two of them looked at each other, both with tears.

"Helen I thought I was losing my mind with the strange dreams. Somehow you put it all together. We've done a lot of good. I think the Richards family may be well. A lot of good Helen. Maybe enough. There is something else."

"I know John, I've been thinking about all of it. God what you did picking up the thoughts of that FBI man, David was it?"

John chuckled for a minute. "Yeah David."

John I didn't help you with that. The chemo therapy seemed to ignite your dreams, but you have a sensitivity, a gift there that is amazing in itself. You knew it was me calling you today."

"Helen it is worse than that. My friend Marty I told you about, he called me today also. I knew it was him calling me. I knew he was beside himself over a first date last night. I knew the girl, the restaurant they went to, the food they ordered, the dress she wore. How do I know these things?" He shook his head, deeply troubled.

"That's the FBI man that used to hound you to work with him isn't it?"

John shook his head and said, "Oh boy."

"What is it?' Helen got after him.

"I'm having dinner with Marty tomorrow night. He's going to be all over me. Helen, our lives crossed again over the Richards case. With my help I guess he wrapped the case all up."

"Well John, maybe there's your answer. I can't go through another night like last night. I just can't."

"Kari makes me want to live. I saw her last night, just briefly. She couldn't see me this time, but when I told her I loved her she knew I was there." John got teary eyed. That always broke Helen up.

"And she told me she loved me. That's the last thing I remember. God I keep going back and forth over this. I can't believe it Helen. She is so beautiful. Wherever she is, I know she is working in some hospital. The doctors must be all over her. I wonder how I could have a chance."

"I've got to tell you something John." Helen was very serious, but seemed very sure of herself. "I need you to believe in this dream. Kari does love you, in whatever way this is all possible. I'm sorry I sure can't tell you what to do. You deserve all the love in the world. I lost her forty two years ago. I am counting. I don't want you wasting your life away. But she has to be the one for you." Helen wept. "She has to be."

John gave her a big hug. "So you're going to tell her that when I bring her to you?"

"I won't have to tell her. Let's just help each other have some faith. I know it's hard."

"When I saw her last night I realized I can't remember how beautiful she is. Memory is not good enough. It is the difference between looking at a sunrise that takes your breath away, and trying to picture it in your mind. You really don't come close. But even in your mind it is the most beautiful thing there is."

"Well you know I'll be praying every day. You have some faith John. Everything happens for a reason."

"She is my reason." The words flowed from John's lips.

Later as Helen drove off John watched the car slowly disappear in the distance. He sat out on his front steps and looked up at the few stars he could see. Once again he let those words flow, "She is my reason."

28

Lead Me Not Into Temptation

John closed the door and put his hand on it for a moment. Somehow the closed door haunted him. "A closed door," he whispered to himself. "What does that mean?"

He cleaned up a few things, pet his cat for a few minutes, and got ready for bed. Before getting in bed he looked out the window. "Seen any owls lately?" he asked Sebastian. He stared out in the distance. He turned around and saw his globe on a table near his desk. He stared at it for a while. "So where is Kari?" He turned the globe slowly, all the way around a few times. Anxiety crept over him. "This is impossible."

Finally in bed he lay there awake, thinking. He even thought to himself he should know better, but he kept thinking. "A man can dream." Sebastian stared at him. He thought to himself, "I see her when I dream. I'm always dreaming when I see her. She is a dream." So much had happened so fast. He could sleep on it, but he wanted to find Kari. He thought about how he had seen her when he was close to death. All the time he had his illness he had expected death. It made him expect death might be the way to Kari. She was his Heaven. Should he try to dream? He didn't understand why he had come close to death. He remembered Helen had said it had been difficult before. Last night was the

159

worst. It had almost killed him. It was the only dream repair since Fusheeswa.

John got up again and paced around his apartment. He looked out the windows several times. He walked out on to the front steps and got some fresh air. He sat back down next to the globe. Finally he lay back down in bed. He felt like his head was a bee's nest, and all the bees were thoughts rushing back in and buzzing around him in a cloud. It was a swarm in his room. "Dam," he got up again and washed his face in the bathroom sink. He dried himself and looked in the mirror. It wasn't such a bad sight. He looked at his reflection and gave himself a talking to.

"You need to get a grip. Think about Helen. What did she say? She needs you to believe in this dream. Even if it is all a waste what you have already seen is more beauty than most people will ever know."

Talking to himself wasn't bad therapy. He pointed at himself in the mirror. "Okay, sleep on it."

He slowly sauntered back into the bedroom. He sat in a chair beside his bed and put his head in his hands. He stayed that way for a while. He didn't know how long. He didn't know what he was feeling, but he suddenly looked to his window again. An owl was watching him. He gasped. It flew away. He opened the window and tried to catch another glimpse. There was nothing. But then a reflection caught his eye. He looked at the window sill. There was a silver heart shaped pendant. He picked it up and brought it over to a light. "Nurses Are Patient People." He stepped outside, looked in all directions, and back at the treasure in his hand. Tears streamed down his face. He kept staring at that pendant. It was a miracle. He knew it. He got down on his knees.

"Kari, Oh my God, I love you. I'm sorry. I will be a patient person. I want to be as beautiful as you. Your mother is always right. I will try to have some faith. I promise."

29

Payday

It was a dreamless night as far as he could remember. John was still taking his vitamins, but not tucking the sheets tightly. He looked over at his bedside table. The pendant was still there. He picked it up and read the inscription again. He remembered Kari explaining it to him. This was another impossible miracle. How could he have this incredible pendant? He kissed it. He thought to himself that he may be quite pathetic, but he is what he is. He could live with it, and there was a lot to suggest Kari could also. He heard purring.

"Good morning Sebastian, I guess I get to enjoy you for another day." The cat jumped up on the bed and was rewarded with scratching behind the ears. "I hope Kari likes cats," John murmured to himself. Sebastian was his only company for now. There seemed to be no way to change that, but John's mind could think of nothing else. He put on some soft music. Chopin's Nocturne Opus 9, #20. It was very soothing. He used to listen to music all the time. It was something to do, and there was nothing more confusing than what he should do. Dinner with Marty should be fun. Eating out in a fine restaurant with a good friend was a wonderful thing to look forward to, and this time he could really enjoy the food. It had been so uncomfortable when he was out with Barbara and Steven. But that had been work. This should be pleasure, but he had to expect Marty would bring up working with him again. It had never been out of the question. He was very interested in the Richard's case. It would be hard to argue with success, but John wanted time. A dream repair is so draining, and how to find Kari was such a challenge. He just had no answers in his life at this point, only questions.

At about ten o'clock the phone rang. John looked at it and his heart started pounding. Susan Richards was calling him.

"Hi it's John," he said.

"John Dreamer, this is Susan Richards." Her voice started to break up. She couldn't hold back the tears.

"Its okay, take your time." John knew this was difficult.

It was nearly impossible for her to speak. "John I needed so badly for you to be for real…and you were. I'm sorry, excuse me." John could hear Susan weeping and blowing her nose.

John tried to help Susan calm down. "My friend Marty told me you and Steven were a very nice couple."

"Oh Marty was amazing. John, Steven and I are going to make it. We're going to make it."

"That's all I hoped for." John felt so good hearing Susan happy. His being was saying a prayer of thanks to God.

Susan regained some composure. "John Danny's in school, Caitlin is in daycare, Steven and I would like to stop by and give you payment. Steven has a figure he wants to suggest. You know we can't put a price on this."

"Yes, billing is the hardest part of the job," John glowed with gratification thinking about Danny and Caitlin getting story time back. He also knew he would have a tough time if people refused to pay. But that was never likely to be an issue. "I'm home all day."

"Is it okay if we come over about eleven?"

"Sure fine. It will be very nice to see you. How is Steven?"

"He is traumatized, hurt, confused, and very sorry. This is like nothing either of us could ever have imagined. You're a miracle. Don't get me wrong, he's also happy. The weight of the world has been lifted from his shoulders. He just feels so bad for letting everybody down."

"We all make mistakes. I wouldn't want to be in his shoes after hurting you and the kids. But he was truly wronged; it was a difficult confusing situation for him."

"We will get past this. Someday we will forget all about it. But we will never forget you. I don't know what to say. It hurts to be so unable to ever thank you enough."

"I think you know your happy family is the best part of payment. I'm sure you and Steven have a reasonable figure for my services. I could only tease about an itemized bill. Maybe when we're old friends I'll send you one as a gag."

"I'd love it. I'd love to be old friends with you. We will be over around eleven o'clock."

"See you then. I'm so glad you sound happy."

"There are no words John. See you soon."

"There are no words," Those words lingered in his mind. Life could be so difficult. He thought to himself how wonderful for Danny and Caitlin to get their father back. Steven had to feel terrible. John had been hard on him, but the kids deserved better and he couldn't let that go. He had to get through to Steven, and it sounded as if it all worked.

Just after eleven the door bell rang. John opened it to see Steven standing next to his wife. "Now that's a handsome couple," John blurted out.

Steven put out his hand. He looked intently into John's eyes. There was some fear, some sadness, but underneath it all a growing happiness. They shook hands and John greeted him warmly. "We meet again under much better circumstances," he looked at Susan, "And with much better company."

"Truer words were never spoken," Steven responded. "John, I don't know what to say. I am so sorry for what I put everyone through."

"A lot of people never learn the lesson Steven. You lost a year.

I couldn't give you that back, but I believed in Susan's dream, and you are that dream. You're a lucky man."

Steven put his arm around Susan. "I've promised not to screw up like that again."

"There are bad people in the world. There are all kinds of sadness. I do believe you can keep it out of your family," John responded.

Susan held up an envelope. She handed it over to John and tears filled her eyes as she spoke. "You know we can't put a price on a second chance for a life together, this can only be a token, but Steven felt it may be proper."

John looked inside the envelope. It was a check for fifty thousand dollars. He assured them it was proper. He looked at them both. "It is impossible for me to set a price, but people do find in their hearts what they need to give."

Steven spoke up, "Susan showed me the business card. Broken Dreams Repaired. The world is stranger than I imagined, but also much better. You saved my life John. That's it in a nutshell. You saved my life. I saw no way out and yet love just sets us free." Steven fought back tears himself.

"I don't think you'll forget it. I better let you two get back to making up for lost time."

Susan spoke up, "I still feel as if I need to do more to thank you. You may hear from us again."

"Just enjoy your family," John beamed. Then he spoke to Steven, "Putting pictures back in your office?"

"Already there." Steven brightened up. John gave him a high five.

John shook Steven's hand again. There were very good vibes. Susan kissed him on the cheek. Sebastian pushed in for some attention and Susan scratched behind his ears for a moment. "Bet the kids would love you."

John laughed, "He's not for sale." He looked at Steven. "You know when you have a keeper."

Steven looked at Susan, "Yes you do. See you around. You be sure to come see me when it is time for you to settle down with your lady friend. We'll find you the right home."

John got that far away look in his eyes. "I'll hang on to that thought."

John sat back in his recliner with a cup of tea. That meeting had gone very well. Whatever else may happen in his life he could know he had made a difference. That is what had been so amazing about dream repair. People can be so close to getting it right, but they can't see the answers right under their noses. They don't seem to believe in their own goodness. And then there are the dark forces that fight against the light. He thought about Marty, dealing with such forces every day. That must be very difficult. How did he always seem to keep a bright attitude? Maybe he would ask him tonight.

Six thirty was fast approaching and John had no easy time finding something to wear. He had lost so much weight as a cancer patient, and for the past month he had been putting it back on. He had to look through older clothes but he finally found something that worked. He spoke to Sebastian, "For a moment there I thought we might have to go to Burger King."

To John's great surprise he was able to tie his tie perfectly on the first try.

"Guess it is like riding a bicycle," he muttered. Suddenly the energy drained from his body. He pictured the blue sign with the bicycle with a line through it to prevent people from riding on the boardwalk. He sat down and put his hands over his face. He remembered the scenes, and he knew Kari was more beautiful than the best his memory could do. He was really always either thinking about her, or trying not to unsuccessfully. How in the world could he find her? He picked up the pendant. It was just such a miracle to have that pendant. It had to be a sign of better things to come. It had to mean it was alright to dream. But it is difficult to have confidence when faced with the absolute impossible.

Suddenly there was a siren out front. Then an FBI megaphone, "John Dreamer, dinner time." John burst out laughing and shook his head. God Marty was a piece of work. He gave the pendant a squeeze in his fist and then placed in down on his nightstand and left the apartment.

He walked down his stairs shaking his head, just looking at that sleek black Lincoln Town Car even made him laugh. Marty rolled the window down. "Need a lift?"

"The neighbors are going to think I'm under arrest," John quipped.

"Ah, you're a criminal like the Green Hornet in this black beauty, actually a crime fighter. I'm Kato, I get to drive." Marty was having fun.

"Martin Douglas you are a piece of work. The biggest one I've ever met in my life." John was actually pretty serious, but this was looking like a great night out. What a need there was for some good clean fun.

The fun was briefly interrupted, and almost lost with their next exchange.

Marty asked, "So you know where we're going?"

John looked intently at Marty with a touch of sadness in his eyes, "The Westchester."

Marty pulled over and looked at John. John continued, "Laurie loved it, her dark blue dress, white pearl necklace and earrings. The seafood platter was to die for."

There was a long moment of silence. Then Marty spoke up, "Are you trying to scare the shit out of me?"

"No, I'm sorry. I may need a new job. I'm trying to impress you."

Marty sat there in silence for another moment, and then he slightly grinned. "Well its working." He floored it and the Town Car burned rubber on the way to the Westchester.

After all the times Marty had been after John to help the bureau John knew he had to be pleased he might get his way. He tried to lighten the mood again and get back on track for a pleasant evening. "Do all the folks with the bureau get a nice car?"

Marty gave John a quick glance, "You work for us I'll give you this car."

"No, you and this car are perfect. Perhaps I could catch a ride now and then."

They pulled up to the elegant Westchester. John couldn't believe he would be eating in a place like this. "This is my first time here by the way."

"I some how knew that," Marty replied. Maybe I have some of your John Dreamer power too."

John looked down. What was this John Dreamer power? Once they were seated and able to relax Marty certainly questioned John about what was going on. What did he mean need another job? What was happening to him that he was so sensitive? Could he just out and out read minds?

John did not have a lot of clear cut answers but he explained as best he knew. He told Marty about how the last dream repair nearly killed him. He intently questioned Marty about how he had handled the Richard's case.

Marty leveled with John. "You know I have been a terrible pain in the ass trying to get you to help us. It was just a thought that your gifts could be put to great use in our field. Well now it is not just a thought. Imagine John the expense of time and resources investigating this Richard's case for eight months. We met with you on a Sunday, and by Monday night it was a done deal. Knowledge is power, great power. I'll give myself a little credit for how I used it. But you are the key to knowledge. So now it is not a theory. Now it is a proven fact you make a difference here. I'm not going to pull any punches John. I love you man. You've made my dream come true. Listen to me, we get child abductions, we get innocent people murdered and we can't give them justice. Mark and Barbara would still be destroying lives. It is certainly not common knowledge, but the FBI will listen to psychics. But John, none of them ever hold a candle to you. I have spoken with David. I sure wish I knew what you did to get him on your side, but I won't go there. David does want you consulting with us, but he insists I'd be stuck with you. He wants no part of it." Marty started laughing. "You're not going to tell me what you did with David are you?"

John laughed, "It wouldn't be proper.

Marty suddenly laughed and pulled out an envelope. "Oh before I forget, I have something for you." He handed it over to John.

"What's this?"

"Open it, go ahead."

John opened the envelope and found a check made out to John Dreamer from the Municipality of Bayside for twenty five thousand dollars.

"What the..." John was speechless.

"You didn't know about this did you?" Marty got a big hardy laugh. "Reward for information leading to the arrest and conviction of those responsible for tampering with a Bayside Elementary School bus."

"Get out of here." John could not believe this.

"They advanced the check on my authority. You've got a lucrative gift there buddy."

"I can't believe this," John just shook his head. "And you're still springing for dinner?"

Marty laughed. "I'm glad I can still surprise you with something. I'm not sure about being friends with someone who can read minds. You better behave. John I have a funny feeling every single person in your life feels they owe you more than they can ever repay. It is not a pleasant feeling."

"I always behave. I'm just so thankful to be alive. And Marty, the Richard's case was mine too. There was no way it would have worked out without you. We are even here."

"Yes," Marty looked intently at John. There was a long moment of silence before Marty spoke again. "It means the world to me to see you looking so well. And that brings us to your girl."

John got the far away look again. Without realizing it he spoke her name, "Kari."

"Kari," Marty spoke it. It jolted John to reality. It seemed strange to hear it come from Marty. "So where is this Kari?"

John looked intensely at Marty. "I have to find her."

What do you know about her?" Marty got after John.

"I know her first name, her mother, her birthday, the hospital, and she must be a nurse." John let the words slip. Marty was the only other person who could know these things.

Marty got intense, "Well John, we can get the mother's DNA and get all this in a national data base. We can find all Kari's in all hospitals."

John got horrified, "No."

Marty pleaded with him. "John I just want to help you. This has to be eating you up. How long have you been looking?"

John looked deep in Marty's eyes. "Marty, please, I'm almost sorry I said anything. This is the most sacred thing in my life. I can't hunt her down like some animal. No tricks. I can't explain it, but you have to trust me. I am dying without her, but the answers have to come to me from a sacred place. I have to be patient."

"John, you always have my highest respect. I'll stay out of this. I just want to be any help I can, always."

"I appreciate that. You're a good friend." John held up his envelope, "Crazy but good." The two of them laughed. John went on to explain that he needed time to sort through everything that had happened. He could envision consulting for the FBI. Mingling with suspects and victims he just may be able to help sense information that could make all the difference. It would be a dramatic new direction, but life seemed to be pointing that way. His last case brought him back to Marty.

It was certainly the best food he had ever eaten outside of Helen's cooking. He was sorry to see the night end. They were pretty quiet for the ride back to John's apartment. The black beauty made for a smooth silent trip. John smirked thinking about it. He did just always pray for his life to count for something. The dream repairs had given him more satisfaction than most people might get in a life time. Helping bring about justice could do the same. Maybe in time he would be a part of that.

They pulled up to the apartment. "Well thanks for the best night out I've ever had." John grinned.

"It was the second best night out I've ever had," Marty responded. "You find Kari and you'll know what I mean."

"I will," John said. He kept trying with all his heart to believe it.

30

What To Do

John woke up the next morning to what would become his usual routine. Other than a large bank deposit his day was quite free. It was a strange feeling. He shook his head in disbelief as he prepared his deposit slip. Life had been an incredible adventure this whole year so far. But what lay ahead? "What shall we do?" He asked. But Sebastian was a typical cat. John chuckled as he really felt thankful for that. He had had absolutely enough strange happenings, and wanted nothing more except what could bring him to Kari. He held the pendant in his hand again with a silent prayer that she was well.

He did his banking and, on a whim, stopped at the coffee shop. He took his fresh cup of coffee to the park and sat on a bench near the gazebo to drink it. It was still quite early in the day. Much traffic was going by as people headed to work, each to their own special place. This was a special place John had found. There were couples walking around the lake. Some elderly folks walked with what must be their grown children. He thought to himself how many of these had been lives well lived. People should be close to one another. It was the beginning of June, but very comfortable. Maybe they would get a break from the heat this year. As he looked at the people walking by he got a good idea. This is where he and Helen should meet for their next

Chinese meal. He would call her later. What an amazing woman she was. He didn't want to let her down. With his coffee finished he decided to walk around the lake a couple of times himself. Walking had often been what kept him sane. His thoughts could clear; the breathing and exercise had to be good for him.

Back at his apartment he called Helen. "How about a Chinese picnic at the park?"

John could sense Helen's smile over the phone. "You pick it up this time. I can't get there until six o'clock, is that okay?"

"Sure Helen."

"How are you doing there John?"

"I guess I'm okay, certainly feeling healthy. I'm just sure perplexed about my next move." John got silent.

"Maybe it's not your move." Helen was as surprised as John at what had slipped out of her mouth. There was silence now as both of them pondered how profound that was.

"Well six o'clock I'll have the perfect picnic waiting. Can't wait to see you." John perked up at the thought.

"Thanks so much John, that's a wonderful idea. I can't wait either. Hope we get good fortunes in our cookies. See you tonight."

John hung up the phone, and once again held the pendant in his hand. Perhaps like Susan's pictures this was something tangible to hold on to in order to believe in your dream.

"Maybe it's not your move," the words echoed in John's head. Helen had saved him so many times he had lost count. Maybe she was saving him again. He was looking forward to seeing her. She was truly family now. He had been through such an emotional roller coaster over the years. The cancer diagnoses, all the stages of grief. Paranormal dreams that allowed him to feel as if he had made a great difference in at least a few lives, and that would trickle out over many. It did his heart such good to think of the Richard's family back together and close as they should be. There would be story time tonight. He remembered Susan confessing how passionate they had been. John was human and healthy. He couldn't help think about pulling Kari close. What could it possibly be like to feel her body against his? Time flew by as such thoughts passed through his mind. Before he knew it he was on his way for Chinese food.

John waited until he saw Helen's car parking along the side of the park before he started to dish the food out of the bag. He had even brought a candle which he lit. As long as there wasn't a breeze it would be a nice touch. Helen was impressed. The two of them greeted with a big hug which was usual now. Neither one wanted to let go.

"This is so nice John, thank you for doing this." Helen was beaming.

"It is my pleasure always." The two of them sat down and started to enjoy the food. "This is the perfect weather for this too," John said with a big smile.

"Looks like you have something on your mind Mr. Dreamer," Helen looked deeply in John's eyes. He had some secret he needed to unload, she could sense that.

John looked intently at Helen, and she could see his eyes start to mist. "I don't know what to do Helen, but I'll sure keep praying and dreaming. I got another miracle last night." He reached in his pocket and got out the pendant. "Please don't ask me Helen, but this belongs to Kari." He handed her the pendant.

Helen read the inscription and wiped tears away from her eyes. "Some of us have these at Bayside Medical. May I wear it until you find her?"

"I have a feeling she will want you to keep it," John was having trouble speaking. It was nothing unusual for those two. They had been through so much together. John shook his head. "We certainly deserve to have something go right Helen. I can't ever think I deserve Kari, but grace is what it is. I've had the dreams. I've tried to follow the signs. I could not be more thankful for how things have turned out for the Richards family. Helen it was another miracle. Somehow we shared in saving a family."

"Oh John it does beat all. After doubting you would live I don't want to be a doubter again. I know you and I have done our best to bring miracles to others. Now it seems like we want our own. I've always wanted this one. Ever since she was born I have needed her, and I've believed she needed me. It has just been so wrong. Hope is a scary thing now. I can't let it eat me up. I have to give it to God. He must know what He's doing. I want to share something I've been reading. I'm sure you've heard it."

Helen got a little Bible out of her purse. "You don't mind if I read something do you?"

"Oh Helen of course not, please do." John felt so touched.

Helen raised up the book. "It is Isaiah Chapter forty verse thirty one." Helen's voice seemed made to read these words. From her it was like listening to a dream. "But they that wait upon the Lord shall renew their strength; they shall mount up with wings like eagles; they shall run, and not be weary; and they shall walk and not faint." Helen reverently lay the book down on the table with her hand over it. John put his hand on hers.

"Thank you so much Helen. I have a feeling Kari is telling me to be patient. I'm sure she would just say have some faith. That is how I knew she was your daughter." John smiled through his misty eyes.

"Have some faith, yes, that is what we need to do. And wait upon the Lord. All things work together for good to them who love Him." Helen smiled. John could not get over what a beautiful woman she was, right to her soul.

"I don't know about you," John perked up, "But I think picnics are a great idea. I'm all for doing this more often."

"Especially with this kind of weather," Helen beamed. "I'm in."

As with the first hug, they didn't want the good-bye hug to ever end. It was so hard to let go. John cleaned up after them, and they drove their separate ways. As John approached his apartment he remembered the fateful night finding Susan there waiting for him. Only Sebastian waited now. There seemed to be a lot of waiting going on. As he walked up his steps he vaguely remembered that his grandfather had written some kind of poem about waiting for love. The thought haunted him. All of his family had passed so long ago, but he remembered a moment when his grandfather had picked him up as a little boy and he thought he could see the whole world from those high shoulders. He had shared a correspondence with his grandfather for a while; there just might be a chance. It was another long shot, but John felt compelled to try. After greeting and feeding Sebastian John dug through his closet and found an old shoe box. There were some letters in it. He took it out and put it on his desk and he looked through each one slowly. One of the letters had that poem.

John got his reading glasses and went over to his recliner. He sat back in a prayerful state of mind and slowly looked at what his grandfather had written so many years ago.

None May Mistake

Let not the least deserving heart despair,
Nor yet be reconciled to compromise;
Love is a miracle we all may share,
There is for each a key to Paradise –
None may mistake or pass the shining gate,
And none are barred but those who will not wait.

John's jaw dropped. It seemed everywhere he looked he was finding miracles. He felt chills so deeply, and he read the words over and over again. His grandfather was amazing. John sat down at his desk remembering how he used to write back and forth to his grandfather. He took a piece of paper and pen, and with a few deep breaths he started to write himself.

"Our lives unfold at their own rate
With guidance from an unseen hand
Our task remains to pray and wait
'Till we look back and understand."

John put his grandfather's poem back in the envelope and placed it on his desk. He sat back down in the recliner in silence, stunned by all that he was thinking. But it was all coming together and making sense. What he had to do, when he was so desperate to do something, anything...was to wait.

31

Good Things Come To Those Who Wait

There really is something special about waking up to purring. As he felt born into each new day John smiled and reached his hand over to the furry head and pointy ears eager for some attention. "I guess I get to enjoy you for another day," He sincerely meant every word. He wondered if Kari had a pet. For his last few years John's life had been defined by his cancer diagnoses. He had read books about the stages of grief. There was no avoiding each stage, but there was some help in understanding that he was not crazy or alone in his circumstances. Now his life had to be redefined, but there would be no books about the stages of a miracle. To his surprise they were much the same.

Shock was understandable, and the temptation to deny that his health was really possible was ever present. He was haunted by the man he and Helen had seen who looked to be just his age, but who was covered over in front of grieving relatives. Why was that not his fate? Guilt easily fit in to the pattern of his thoughts. But why should he be burdened with any of this in the first place? People do not go through this kind of thing. He could feel himself resentful, but then realize what awe had been the reality for he and Helen as powers he could not explain let him make a difference in the lives of very decent people. John, with Helen's help, had made all the difference in several very important lives. He could not be more thankful than to play any part in helping the Martys and Susans of the world. And just dreaming of Kari made him the luckiest man in the world. So his feelings of depression seemed out of place, yet he did have to deal with that. Perhaps whatever waiting he would have to endure was necessary because he was not ready for Kari. That thought shocked him, but it also woke him up. He better get ready, and that would be a later stage in the miracle process. It seemed obvious when he really looked at it.

To just wait might have done him in, but the thought of getting ready made life a blessing. He only had to battle his own doubts. Fixing up his apartment so it could accommodate a wondrous lady was a very positive chore, as was shopping for clothes which would fit him properly. Getting involved in such projects did lead him to a stage of hope. Helen was glad to be a part of giving his home a woman's touch, helping him pick out some clothes that wouldn't be an embarrassment. There were some fun moments through that month of June, and through July.

One morning as John put on a sweat suit and started outside for a power walk he ran into his neighbor Joe.

"John?" Joe asked, as if unable to believe his eyes.

"Hey Joe, great to see you."

Joe smiled but was determined to bust John's chops. "You know, you look somewhat like a guy John who used to live here, but he was skin and bones, always going to the hospital. Funny I haven't heard from him lately. I used to watch his cat."

John raised his hands as if under arrest. They both beamed as they shook hands. John told Joe, "Man, you were a life saver. How many times was it?"

"I lost count. Lucky for you Sebastian is such a sweet one. How is the big devil?"

"Still the sweetest. I hit the jackpot with that cat."

"So how can you be looking so fit? This is unbelievable," Joe was amazed as well he should be.

"Modern medicine, what can I tell you? And I know I've got the greatest nurse in Bayside."

"Well I won't keep you from your exercise. It has made my day to see you looking so fine. I'm so glad to hear it John. I didn't want to lose a good neighbor."

"Thanks Joe. I've got the best neighbor."

Walking had always helped John cope with whatever was on his mind. It felt so good to be healthy. "They shall run and not be weary," Helen's reading echoed through his head. But there was depression, and there still was doubt. Sensitivity seemed to be his gift, but at times he felt a vulnerability he wished he could shake. He felt his emotions deeply, and memories and other triggers could make him feel as if he was braking. So much brought him back to his raw emotion of needing Kari. Seeing other couples at the park while he walked alone, just a bicycle reminding him of the blue sign, a green lizard in an auto insurance commercial... these things could make him weep before he knew what hit him. He preferred when it wasn't in public, but didn't feel inclined to fight it anywhere.

For Helen's part, she wished to cope with all that had happened and all that would happen through prayer. Helen did consider herself the Lord's servant. Fearing John's death had broken her spirit and destroyed her faith. She struggled with guilt over that, but knew with Fusheeswa the love of God had the final word. She needed to cling to that. As saintly as she may be it could be said she was guilty of one flat out crime. It did seem as innocent as could be, but her own behavior shook her up. About two years ago she had been going through John's chart when she came across his insurance card and driver's license. With the office completely to herself she had copied his driver's license, blown up the picture, and shredded the rest. So she did have in her possession a small black and white photo of John. She put that picture with a statue of Mary and a candle in her private study where she would kneel to pray. It helped her focus to see the image of John, yet she could not escape some guilt over how she obtained the photo. She promised God she would replace it when possible and asked to please be allowed this borrowing so she could pray better for this special man.

During the last week of July John took one trip to the Jersey Shore. It wasn't far for him to go. He did not wish to get drawn into the crowds or commercialism, but sought out a place where he could be alone with the Atlantic Ocean. It seemed strange in a way that one really could just walk away from the crowd. He might be getting on private land but he walked where he felt led. He was intent on the waves, the shells, and all the gifts of the sea. When he stopped to get his bearings, he discovered he was the only one he could see. He knelt down in the sand and let the ocean waves wash up against him. There were some shore birds and crabs scooting across the sand. The ocean was a part of the great mystery of life, and John felt so humble there in the sand. He was always more inclined to give than to ask for anything, but there was one prayer that came to him without choice. "Please let me find her."

The last day of July gave no indication it would be different from any other day, but perhaps hotter. It was a Friday, but Helen was off work because she would be working that weekend at the hospital. So she invited John over for lunch. "See you later buddy," John said as he massaged Sebastian's head and ears, "You spoiled thing."

John was amused to think his car could almost automatically head to Helen's house now. He shook his head in consideration of how grateful that made him feel. He chuckled at the thought perhaps the greatest miracle he could receive was a decent mother-in-law. Life was certainly an interesting "Kettle of fish," as his mother used to say so long ago.

Along the route John drove by Richard's Realty. The sign was down and there was some construction equipment along the property. That was the last thing John expected to see and he found it quite unsettling. He had had no contact with the Richards family, but certainly thought this was a dream repair that had gone well. What could this mean?

John tried not to let his concern detract from his wonderful lunch with Helen, but she could also sense things well, especially with John. "Alright, what is eating you Hun?" Helen got after him.

"Well, I passed Richard's Realty and there was some construction equipment, the sign was down. I don't know what is going on," John replied.

"Well you can pick up the phone and ask them. They're your realtors. You and Kari should have a bigger place." Helen did her best to keep positive, but her tears betrayed how hard she was wishing inside. John felt her pain.

"I just may do that. You are a wise woman dear lady. No sense in fretting all day. Maybe I'll stop by on my way home." John tried to pick up their mood. He asked to see the pendant again. Having that precious piece of jewelry was like having a jolt of hope. "I have to confess Helen that I just keep loving her more and more each day. But it is a hard love to fathom. I thought of how precious you are on my way over here, but the blessing of being in your company is ten times better than I can imagine. I don't know how I could handle the real flesh and blood Kari in my life, let alone my home." It was difficult for John to say.

Helen actually perked up. "You find my Kari and mister you are going to forget everything. You are going to forget to breathe. Everything will be fine in spite of yourself. You just have some faith there."

John raised his eyebrows, "Well now you're talking."

Visits with Helen were never long enough. John just didn't feel like facing the Richard's family that day, but he drove by the business again. Something was going on. He hoped everything was okay, but he wanted to leave any worry over that for another day.

John did stop for a cup of coffee at the convenience store. He remembered the fateful meeting with Dr. Brady. He decided to pick up a local newspaper. "It never hurts to know what is going on in the world," He said quietly to himself. But news was often about broken or breaking dreams. John was somewhat haunted by what to do. He still thought of dreaming, and it could still happen anyway.

As the day turned into night John found himself becoming fragile. He hated the feeling but he couldn't change it. Helen was the dearest sweetest lady he could ever know. He just wanted to bring Kari to her and watch their dream be healed. He so wanted Helen to get all the happiness she had been missing for a lifetime. He hoped it could mean the same for Kari. This was not a selfish wish. John couldn't help reminding God of that. Even if Kari didn't love him as he dreamed he needed to do this for Helen and Kari. But John could hear Helen's voice scold him, and tell him how much he would be loved. He was going to be swept off his feet big time. He wiped away a tear.

John sat back in his chair and opened the paper- and there was a shocker. John turned to a full page add for Richard's Realty. They were changing their name to "Richard's Family Realty." John read the ad. Steven and Susan were making it their mission to find a home for your family. There was a large portrait of the Richard's family, obviously recently taken at a studio. The entire family glowed with a love you could feel coming out of the newspaper. "Holy..." was the only word John could speak. As he looked at the expression on Caitlin's face as she smiled at her mother John could only feel a crushing need to bring Kari to Helen. More tears came. "Please," John cried. It was not clear if he was pleading for his tears to stop or for the miracle to come.

The door bell rang. It jolted John out of what had become a kind of trance. He grasped for his bearings. It was 8:45PM at night. Who on earth could be ringing his doorbell at this time?

John opened the door to find Susan Richards standing there. He couldn't be more shocked. "Susan," He called out, "Is everything alright?"

Susan glowed. "Oh John, everything is so alright except for one thing. That's why I'm here." John noticed she held some kind of large package.

"Is there anything I can do?" John pleaded out of his concern.

"John, the one thing that is making this all so difficult for me is that there is just no way I can thank you. I know you were paid, I know you are a good man and you just want to see us happy. But John you saved my life. You honestly saved my life John Dreamer. I've asked all of Heaven what I can possibly do to let you know how much you mean to me and my family, and how I can possibly feel I've thanked you. I know it may seem so silly, but I felt I needed to make this for you. It helped heal me in the process, Steven loved it, we have a copy ourselves. I want you to have this please." She offered John the package.

"Wow Susan I love your family, and you know I don't need any more thanks, but thank you so much for thinking of me." John was absolutely astonished.

"I've got to go," Susan turned to leave. "We will never ever forget you John."

"Thank you," John yelled out. "Give my best to everyone."

John stood there in his doorway holding his fairly heavy package and watching Susan drive away. He looked again at the license plate, "Real T." He grinned.

"Wow," He said. He would have to share this with Sebastian, whatever it was. He sat down in his recliner with this package in his lap and carefully started to unwrap it. The wrapping paper was beautiful flowers and inside was a white box. He slowly opened it. Inside he found green tissue paper. There was lots of green tissue paper. It was a hot night. His window was open and a breeze started blowing across the room. He lifted up sheet after sheet of this green paper that waved across him as a curtain. The last sheet he gazed through at what was in the box. Chills came over him as he gazed through this green curtain listening to the growing wind. The sound seemed to come from everywhere.

It was a photo album. Susan had worked this one to perfection. Beautiful gold lettering spelled out, "A Dream Repaired."

John set the tissue paper beside him and opened the album. There were three sections, Love, Marriage, and Family. He very slowly, carefully turned the first page. There were photos of Steven and Susan in high school. "High school sweethearts" was a label on a perfect picture of those two. John could lift the pictures out and look on the back of each one where Susan had written some description. "Steven & Susan, class of 1995." This was so touching to John. What an incredible way to look at a dream repaired. He loved the courtship pictures. Envied the love they shared. Photos of them dancing, swimming, kissing, playing with a whole bunch of puppies, horse back riding.

Next he came to the section on Marriage. He started to open that up, but he got two pages at once, the wind picked up and blew the green tissue paper back across the album, and John again looked through it. This time what he saw gave him chills like he had never felt in his life. He shivered violently in the recliner. Through the green he could see a boardwalk with mist and ferns. He pulled the tissue paper away. There was a photo of Susan beside the blue sign- a bicycle with a line through it. "Oh my God," John broke down. He had to put the album down. He was hyperventilating, and he couldn't chance his tears damaging any photos. "Oh my God," He nearly screamed. Sebastian ran under the bed. John paced back and forth and went in the bathroom to wash his face in cold water. He stepped outside for a breath of fresh air. It had to be ninety degrees but he went back inside and put on a thick bathrobe. When the tears subsided enough he sat back down with the album. He could see a picture of the waterfall where he had taken Fusheeswa. He turned the page back to see what he had missed. "Our Honeymoon." There was Steven beside a huge national park sign. "Cascade River State Park," Minnesota.

John was back in the bathroom rinsing his face over and over, and trying to catch his breath. He would wait all night if he had to for his tears to stop. Finally back at the album he kept going. There were photos of the stairs. Susan was at the top of a flight of stairs. John counted the twenty five stairs. He blurted out the words over and over, "Cascade River State Park, Oh my God." He went back outside and paced a few times back and forth in front of his apartment. Then back to that album. There was a photo of Steven holding a green lizard he had caught. There were photos of the colorful mushrooms, slate outcrops, and ferns, Steven in front of stairs and waterfalls, Susan in front of stairs and waterfalls. Finally at the bottom of a page was a photo of Steven and Susan together in front of the largest waterfall at the top of the stairs, right where Kari had been. It took John a moment to grasp that this was a photo of both of them. Somebody had to have taken this picture. He absolutely held his breath and turned the page. He saw the photo for just a moment before he had to give up again. Back to the bathroom to wash his face a few more times, and remind himself to breathe.

Back at the album he finally faced this last photo in this section. It was Kari standing by the waterfall. John carefully lifted the photo and looked at what Susan had written. "Our guest photographer Kari, nursing student from Duluth, August 14th, 2000."

"I've got you!" John cried out to Kari. "I've got you!" August 14th was two weeks away and John knew Kari would be at Cascade River State Park in Minnesota, and he would be there to get her.

John stared at the photo, ten years younger, but there she was. She was so gorgeous. There was nothing he had ever seen that could compare. He placed the album against the back of the recliner and kneeled before Kari. "I will always love you 'till my last breath and beyond."

Without a thought he dialed Helen's number. It was after midnight by now, but what could matter?

"Hello," The dazed half asleep Helen spoke into the phone.

"Helen," John spoke her name but lost the ability to speak.

"John?" Helen asked with concern.

"Duluth." It took everything John had for him to be able to say that name.

"Oh my God John," Helen broke up as she knew John was broken.

"Yes," John cried. "I know Helen, I know."

"John," was all she could say.

"I've got her. Helen…" this was all beyond words.

After a long silence John said to Helen, "I'll need you to watch Sebastian."

The tension finally eased. A gentle laughter brightened their lives like the most beautiful dawn. "We can talk about everything tomorrow," Helen spoke as well as she could through all those tears.

"You mean later," John also spoke through what was left of his tears. He had never been so cried out in all his life. "Goodnight."

"Very goodnight," Helen hung up the phone.

John could not tear his eyes away from Kari. John remembered every word Kari had spoken, "I need you more than anything."

He looked at that photo and prayed to Kari, "I can't kid myself. I need you more than anything. I don't know how you can be who you are, but I will worship the ground you walk upon and lift you up and carry you home."

32

August 14th

The two weeks went by in a flash. Getting the car tuned up, packing, praying, and dreaming. So often in his life John had felt that he wasn't just living, but being led. It was never more certain than now.

John opened his eyes. The LED display on the radio by his bed read 4:55AM, the alarm was set for 5AM. John turned it off. He lay there in that bed, in a small motel in Lutsen Minnesota. It had taken him three days to drive there. Life had taken on such a surreal dreamlike quality. But this was no dream. John had to keep telling himself it was no dream. He almost spoke that out loud. To embrace the reality of it all he was super focused on the physical, and on his physical senses. He felt the bed linen underneath him, the soft pillow that had held his head. He smelled the sheets, the air freshener that had been used on that room, the pine scent coming in through an open window. Soon he felt the hot water streaking over his body, smelled the soap, the shampoo, he tasted the tooth paste. He missed the feel of Sebastian's head under his fingers, and the sound of purring. He hoped Helen was enjoying that sweet animal.

The aroma of coffee and the hot feel of it on his lips were comforting. He had been able to bring about dream states where he was awake. This was an awake state where he was dreaming.

That is what it felt like. Showered, groomed, and dressed, he checked out of the motel before 6AM. It would not be a long drive, but it would burn into his memory forever. The early morning mist was beautiful. The sun across the tops of trees was a perfect picture. He had seen a black bear just before arriving at the motel yesterday. This morning a huge bird gliding across a blazing sunrise must be a Bald Eagle. Kari was everywhere, in everything. Once he crossed into Minnesota he couldn't help feeling almost paranoid. She could be anywhere. She could have been in the next room last night, or at the next gas station or restaurant. Hope was heavy, and he didn't know how long he could carry it.

It seemed like a long time, but also like just a moment. The beautiful sign read, "Cascade River State Park." John had been listening to the physical sound of his car engine running. It was dramatic when he turned the engine off. He could hear his breathing; feel his heart pounding in his chest.

He stepped out of his car and shut the door. The physical sound of the door slam was intense, as was the quiet that followed. There were no other cars yet. If Kari would come he wanted to be at the top of the falls. He couldn't hear the water yet, but there were some high-pitched song bird sounds. It was a cool morning, but clear and beautiful. The coolness would help for the long walk and the stairs that lay ahead.

The path into the park started out rather rugged. Countless pebbles across the Minnesota ground paved his journey. The trail led downward first, and after about 10 minutes he was in the mist as it had been in his first dream. He could not see his feet, but he bent down and scooped up the moist ground. He felt it in his hand. He brought it up to his nose and smelled it. He could feel cool moisture, and see his hands draw the mist slowly before him. Walking on for another few minutes he heard the water. It was eerily familiar, coming from everywhere. He stroked his hands along the fern leaves, and picked one to hold. He stopped and stared at it for a while. It was a beautiful green, damp with morning dew, and cool to the touch. It was difficult to take in that this was really happening. It all seemed so impossible on the one hand, and just too easy on the other. Anyone could just come here, but it was a miracle when he did. But the chill though his whole body was the growing possibility that this would be the day that would define his life from now on.

His feet reached the beginning of the boardwalk. John still had his incredible health. Every day he woke up to it and gave thanks. It was enough of a miracle that he had lived this long. "What is a miracle?" He spoke to himself as he often did. He came to the blue picture of a bicycle with a line though it and answered his own question. "This."

He stared at the sign. He put his hand on it. It was real, and like everything else it was damp. Susan had stood right here, and so had Kari. John had been here first in a dream, but now he held it in his hands. He couldn't care how it must look to anyone else. "I'll never have to pray for a sign as long as I have this one." It was difficult to take his eyes off it and move on. He put his hand on the post and squeezed it. He felt the hard wood.

As he ascended along the boardwalk he approached the first set of stairs. "I can see why I needed perfect health." John grabbed the railing. He crushed it with his hand, or tried to. The feel of the hard wood clarified everything was still real. He would get a splinter if he wasn't careful. Up and up and up he climbed, looking at the rock formations, the plants, the colors, and an occasional frog. He saw the sign warning against taking anything natural out of the park. He sometimes looked back. If Kari was following she would have time to catch up. The thought fit the pounding of his heart. Her car might be next to his in the parking lot right now. Maybe he should turn around and run back. Maybe he should have stayed home. But life for John had become a dream that possessed him, and he had only to follow where it led. This place was worth the trip.

He shook his head as he climbed stair case after stair case, heard more birds as the forest came to life, discovered rainbows where the rising sun woke up the cascades. Finally, it was that last stretch of boardwalk. At the end of the railing he saw the owl. It took off to leave him to his dream. He gazed intently as it glided soundless into the tall pines and disappeared. He stood by the falls right where Kari had stood, and sat down where she had sat. He looked at the falls. It was an awesome sight. No wonder she stared at it. John stood up and looked at how far he could fall if he went over the railing. He better be careful. He had family now. Helen had become closer than any family had ever been. She must be on edge back home, but nothing compared to John. He practically shivered. The nerve chill factor he called it. He had done everything in his power, and some things that were not. This was where he needed to be. John sat back down in that magical place and waited. It didn't take long.

From time to time he would peek down the stair cases as far as the eye could see. It may have been a half hour, maybe not even. There was somebody coming. This place was too beautiful to keep to one's self, but there was only one person he wanted to share it with. "Time for the impossible," he heard himself say. He looked down at this figure approaching slowly up the stairs. "My God." Tearing up, John sat and clutched his seat. He focused on his breathing. He felt the cool mist of the falls, listened to the water rushing over the rocks, and saw the love of his life step onto the other end of this boardwalk.

He wondered if he was invisible. If so his breathing would give him away. Could this possibly be real? Could she see him?

She brought her hands to her lips as if surprised to find someone there. Someone was in her spot. But one can't expect to have Heaven all to herself, and maybe by one's self it isn't Heaven. She sauntered ever so slowly over toward John. She stopped just a few feet away. John caught himself staring, just as in the dream, but it was just as helpless to resist. He noticed she had been crying.

He wouldn't be one to talk. He wiped a quick tear out of his eye. God she was so beautiful. He just kept praying that this was real. As their eyes met it felt to both of them as if they were just learning to see. There was an overwhelming awe, thick and heavy. Their faces were like sunshine to each other. An impossible recognition was taking place. Each was seeing a dream come true. Their eyes locked under the spell of everything that was meant to be. Nothing had ever felt like this. If it had been night they might have seen each other glow.

Kari stood before him, looking at him in obvious shock, but he couldn't know why. "Oh my God," she exclaimed.

"Yeah," he replied, grinning, shaking his head. "Kari," John spoke out as he gazed into those magical eyes.

She held up her hands, palms facing John, thumb tip to thumb tip- looking at him as if he was framed in a picture. "John, tell me you are John."

"How do you know this?" John was beside himself.

"How did you know my name?" Kari asked. She grinned. John was dying, but in a good way.

"I have been given a gift of dreaming. It was in a sacred dream that I found you, spoke to you, and you asked me to find your name. You told me to find you. I gave my life to that task. Nothing else could matter to me; he paused for a moment, except your mother."

Kari put both of her hands over her mouth. John could see the tears begin to fall. He gazed at her with all his love.

"Knowing your mother taught me who you were. She knew your name." John could only look at her in wonder.

Kari's eyes glowed through her tears. They were the deepest blue he had ever seen.

"My mother," Kari spoke the words dreaming this was real.

John nodded, giving her the assurance this was okay. As she looked at John it reminded him of how his barber looked at him, as if he was about to create his look or was admiring his own handiwork.

"John," she spoke, and he closed his eyes just to perceive more fully the sound of her voice. The sound of her speaking his name went straight to the depths of his heart and would stay there forever. He would play it over and over if any dark time ever came again. But this gift of being with Kari made Heaven real, and eternal. Nothing could take this away from him, ever.

Kari continued, "All my life I have loved to draw. The pictures come to me. I feel them to be a gift, and that my hand draws by some guidance I can't understand. I've been alone most of my life. I knew I was adopted. It was an older couple, both gone now. They always encouraged me in everything, my art, nursing school, and my dreams. I have a gift for you, lots of gifts." A look of wonder, awe, fear, and John could dare hope love shined from her face.

She had a satchel over her right shoulder. She took it off and opened it, lifting out a sketch pad. She looked intently at what she had drawn. Tears started flowing from her eyes.

"Kari," John spoke her name, and he too shed tears at just the sound of it along with the wonder that she was right there.

She turned the pad so John could see. It was unmistakably a picture of him. John wiped away his tears and nodded his head looking at Kari. They stared at each other in silence and awe until finally Kari could speak.

"What else did you dream?" She asked.

John looked at Kari standing while he was still sitting beside the falls. He had been unable to move, but now he would live his dream. "Kari," he said, and he felt his strength grow. "You can come closer." It was a declaration both of them could share.

"I guess I can," she beamed.

There was a silence except for the water. John looked at her with his whole heart. He reached out his hand, motioned her to take it and sit with him. Their hands joined, and there was that feeling only the luckiest lovers will ever know.

"I had been very ill Kari. You mother is the best of nurses, but I was slipping away until I met you in a dream. You knew I was sick. You gave me the medicine that saved my life."

Kari squeezed his hand and looked at him shaking her head. "What medicine did I give you?" John shut his eyes again. He breathed in the sound of her voice.

"Fusheeswa." John opened his eyes to see the astonished look on her face. It seemed every emotion at once was coming out. Realizing he held her hand in his it was all he could do to believe what he was feeling. He thought for a moment about this connection being both ways. Could she "see" how much he loved her? He quickly realized just how silly that thought was. It would not take any powers to see that. John actually laughed for a moment at his silliness.

"What?" Kari grinned. It was Heaven.

John spoke out, "I can't hide what you know how to see."

"Fusheeswa?" Kari looked at John like she had him in her sights.

It was always a most sacred confession to speak that word.

"Fusheeswa." John said it for all it was worth.

Kari was astonished to be sure, but she was also suddenly shy and embarrassed. It seemed like she was teasing when she spoke to him again.

"You mean to tell me I gave you Fusheeswa?"

If John was pegged for something he didn't know what. "In my dream," He whispered. His voice had weakened.

Kari laughed. It was so precious, but John couldn't imagine why.

"In your dreams," Kari spoke it as people do when someone has asked for too much. The two of them sat there locked in each other. John felt they had to love each other, but it seemed he had been taken down a notch.

"Do you know what Fusheeswa is?" Kari asked him.

"I only know it is what I needed to save me, and you gave it to me." He humbly shrugged, "Thank you."

Kari laughed and cried at the same time, and she looked at this man who had found her. He was the man who had haunted her in her dreams. He knew her mother. She thought of what he must have gone through to find her. He was a precious man.

"I'll tell you what it is John." It was an awesome moment of anticipation. Kari was so beautiful it almost hurt to look at her. John wondered how long this could last, but it better be at least a life time.

"It is all the love a person has. All of it."

Kari was even beautiful through the countless tears that streamed out of John's face as he tried to take it all in. He nodded and smiled, and there was something about him that seemed as innocent as a little boy hoping to open the door to Christmas.

"You want to know something else?" Kari looked at him, and there was all the love of dreams glowing right there.

"What?" John asked, bracing himself.

Kari squeezed his hand, and took his breath away with everything he could hope for.

"You still have it."

Time usually runs from moment to moment, minutes, hours, days, years. But as the two of them held each other there was nothing time could do. Tears replaced words; emotions replaced the air they breathed. Love was everything.

33

One Year Later

John approached the refrigerator in their new home. He gazed at the Richard's Family Realty calendar attached to the front. He looked again at the love in that family. He felt Sebastian push his head into his leg. "Well Buddy, I guess we get to enjoy you for another day." John had spoken very quietly to not wake up Kari yet.

He circled the day on the calendar, August 14th. He looked at the package he had put at Kari's place at the table. They would have so many anniversaries, but this was a special one. He stood there as if in a trance remembering that precious day one year ago. It seemed like only a moment could have passed. He watched in his mind's eye as he and Kari had risen for their first long beautiful walk. Arm in arm they would so slowly weave their way back through that park, and out into a new life. He grinned as he remembered the few times they put their hands in the cold waterfalls and sprinkled each other. That was the most Holy baptism. He saw himself point out to her the waterfall where he had taken his medicine. He asked her to stand by the blue sign for a moment, and he put his hands out thumb tip to thumb tip framing her in that picture. They shared such precious laughter. He had followed her to her apartment. It was precious and comfortable, but astonishing for the drawings which decorated each wall. John had no family pictures to remind him of his youth, but all these drawings Kari had done over the years were his life. No one could mistake the resemblance. Just as his dreams had crossed the given barriers of what men know, Kari's love formed a door only he could walk through.

He remembered their astonishing conversation. "When did you start drawing..." John could hardly speak it, "Me?"

Kari spoke up in a lively tone, "I remember exactly when it was, May 3rd 2005. I felt possessed, took up the pad and drew like my life depended on it, and there you were."

May 3rd 2005, it was a day John knew well. It was the day of his first appointment with Dr. Bernard, and his first contact with Helen Weiss. Couples in their bond of love do create each other through everything they share, yet he and Kari had created each other before any chance to meet. She was a creation of his dreams; he was a creation of her artistic gifts.

They didn't even kiss that first day. Togetherness was complete without any sign necessary. The next morning waking up to her would be a different story.

He slept on the couch. "John," she ran her fingers through his hair waking him that next morning. "I have a question for you."

Waking up to Kari could not be beat by going to Heaven as all the stories had promised.

"What?" John beamed.

"Is there such a thing as soul mates?" Kari looked at him like she knew the answer.

John grinned and glowed as he thought to himself, "No pressure there." But he had his answer. He sat up and gazed in those magical eyes and gave her his answer. "There is now."

She was all over him after that, and in his present moment-that kiss was all he could remember of an entire year. But Kari's present would bring the rest back. He couldn't wait for her to open it. He turned on the coffee maker, and after a few minutes took a magazine and fanned the aroma toward their bedroom. "That will get her," He winked at Sebastian.

She appeared in the doorway. "Always an apparition," John shook his head. Kari glowed, "Ditto."

"Happy anniversary," Kari embraced John as Sebastian ran under the bed. If the cat could speak it would be repeating, "There they go again," several times throughout each day. If love is supposed to mellow into familiarity it wasn't happening for these two. John would never forget that living is a blessed gift. Kari would never forget that some people are without family, lost ever wondering and wishing for some elusive dream they would call love. The sad fact is people throw it away. John and Kari would make no mistakes.

"What's this?" Kari asked as she saw the gift at her place.

"Well it's our anniversary," John answered.

"But you first," Kari opened a cabinet door and got out a beautifully wrapped present for John.

"Wow," he laughed. "You remembered."

"Silly you," Kari let him have it.

John opened his present, a beautifully wood carved owl. It was so perfect. It was another excuse to escape time in a kiss.

Finally Kari sat down to open her gift. She carefully tore off the paper and removed the lid. There was a lot of green tissue paper covering this wonder. She knew the story, and looked at John through a sheet of it. They were all grins.

"I had some help with it," John confessed.

"Oh John," Kari teared up. It was a photo album, very beautifully done with gold lettering. "Our First Year," was the title. It would be a very good morning. They sat together with their coffee and relived what seemed to be only a moment ago. These two had been making up for lost time. It was the greatest gift they could give each other, making up for lost time. So it was a thick album. There were pictures of John and Kari at Niagara Falls, John and Kari at Cider Mills in Vermont, An aquarium in Connecticut, the zoo in Philadelphia, riding horses in the Poconos. They laughed at one that showed the two of them riding a lion statue in some museum.

That was a special twist to this album. These were pictures of both of them together. They didn't have to take turns with a camera, and as a result what they saw was their life together in love as they are. It was all possible because they did have their own photographer. And there she was in the last picture, the best photographer and the happiest Mom the world had ever known.

John and Kari huddled together, thankful for every minute of it all. John handed her a poem he had written. "Just trying to find some words for you," he said.

Can't Look Away

I've always been the shy man,
Besides, it's not polite to stare…
So no matter how beautiful,
No matter how much love
I have ever felt for anyone…
I just enjoyed those quick glances.

But you…
I looked at you and I saw-
Something I have never ever seen before…
Eyes loving me.
I did not know what that looked like,
There was no way I could know…
And I was trapped in Heaven
And could not look away.

Thank you for giving me
What I never had,
And teaching me
What I could never learn
Without you…
It is polite to stare when dreams come true.

By John H. Bidwell

About the Author

John Bidwell has held a number of different positions in healthcare administration over the course of his career, most notably with Kessler Rehabilitation Center. He has also served as Facility Manager for Our Lady of Sorrows Convent in Denville NJ.

During his freshman year in high school John discovered a love for writing poetry which has continued through his life.

John's grandfather Leonard W. Bidwell wrote poetry through his entire life, passing away in 1984. Because it was possible, and above all so deeply appropriate, in the later portion of this book

John incorporated his grandfather's poem "None May Mistake" into this story. It fits and will serve as a tribute to this special man in John's life.

In 2008 ideas for a novel started haunting John, leading him to write Fusheeswa.

Printed in the United States
By Bookmasters